PRAISE FOR *NEON MOON*

"The blood flows faster than the whiskey in *Neon Moon*, a brutal ballad with lively characters who will two-step their way into your heart. Grace R. Reynolds serves up a rootin'-tootin' hackin'-slashin' good time!"

—Brian McAuley, *USA Today*-bestselling author of *Breathe In, Bleed Out*

"Drenched in poetic prose and a whole lotta whiskey, *Neon Moon* is one of the best slashers I've read in a while. It's an absolute thrill ride. Reynolds has crafted a killer that makes Leatherface look like a puppy."

—Emily Ruth Verona, author of *Midnight on Beacon Street* and *Shiva*

"The jukebox runs red in this deep-fried slasher that twists horror tropes like a do-si-do. With *Neon Moon*, Reynolds gives us an intelligent genre exercise that mixes survivor narrative and revenge thriller with buckets upon buckets of blood."

—Joey Powell, author of *Night Games* and *Squirming All the Way Up*

"*Neon Moon* is the honky-tonk bridal-shower slasher of your nightmares. Reynolds offers a *Roadhouse*-meets-Leatherface mashup with a Western final girl who literally gives the patriarchy the axe."

—Wendy Dalrymple, author of *Bed Rot Baby* and *Killer Summer*

"Grace R. Reynolds takes you by the wrist and drags you through the mud, blood, and dark liquor that swirls through the veins of *Neon Moon*. She deftly captures the essence of Texas and the gritty, leathered souls that populate these pages. Every step into the Teegarden brings with it a shot of rattlesnake venom, so please dear reader, be ready for the burn."

—Jeremy Megargee, author of *Soulmates, Crown of Carrion,* and *These Words Leave Scars*

"Soaked in sin, *Neon Moon* is brilliant, chilling, and delightfully bloody. It's the perfect Texas slasher, with brutal twists and turns that will have your jaw on the floor, gripping the pages until the very end. Every gruesome encounter is interwoven with lush description that truly showcases Reynolds's poetic skill, adding a dreamy, dizzying layer to the carnage."

—Sirius, author of *Rising Sun Over the Devil's Nest*

"*Neon Moon* is a briskly paced slasher, featuring memorable characters, a western saloon dripping with nostalgia, and a twist that arrives like a jump scare in the heat of the night."

—Kayli Sholz, author of *Saint Grit, Black Rain Season, and Yeehaw Junction*

NEON MOON

Edited by Rob Carroll
Book Design and Layout by Rob Carroll
Cover Art by Katerina Belikova
Cover Design by Rob Carroll

Library of Congress Control Number: 2026935960

ISBN 978-1-958598-96-2 (paperback)
ISBN 978-1-958598-64-1 (eBook)

darkmatter-ink.com

NEON MOON

GRACE R. REYNOLDS

DARK
MATTER
INK

To those who yearn for the open road in search of home.
Keep driving. The view gets better.

AUTHOR'S NOTE

AS AN AUTHOR, I understand and want to be mindful of themes in this book that may be unsettling for readers. I want readers to enjoy *Neon Moon,* but not at their personal expense! For a complete list of trigger warnings, please check the copyright page of this book.

Thank you!
Grace

LOSS OF THRUST

DEATH IS A flightless bird. Her wings are clipped, and she struggles to flutter off the ground. She is the warbler hiding in low brambles as the hungry fox approaches. Watching. Waiting. Her tiny heart beats furiously in its breast to the rhythm of night. A cacophony of cicadas screaming a crescendo signals the hunt's final act.

If the warbler stays where she's at she will die. If she runs, he will chase her. Outrun her. Push her down, break her neck, and finish what he started. A deep gash in her thigh sends a shock wave down to her toes, the damaged nerve pulsating like heat lightning in the clouds above. The effects of adrenaline slowly wearing off makes her acutely aware of the pain and how dire her situation is.

She's tired. So very tired. The warbler doesn't know how much blood she's lost on her descent down the hillside. She's lightheaded, weak, and nauseous. If she could find a place to hide, die in peace—fall away in solitude like the dying animal that she is—she would. Anything would be better than succumbing to the terror following her tracks.

A legato of grunts approaches from behind. Running won't save her. She must take flight.

The sound of her tiny feet rustling through the underbrush are the trebles of mallets against timpani. Her eyes scan the woods, but it's no use. Scraggly tree limbs play tricks, create shapes, deceive and whisper between rustling oak leaves. The warbler will not find coverage behind the dancing trunks of junipers. Not in the way she needs them to. Her breast heaves, out of breath and threatening misstep, and the warbler plunges deeper into the forest. Sobs escape her throat, doing nothing to conceal her.

Her soles cry out in agony as her foot plants perfectly on the pointed edge of a rock, first hobbling her and then sending her tumbling forward. Wet leaves and fallen sticks brush against her skin, scratching her arms as her face makes impact against a small boulder. Roots detach, sending teeth flying into the fermentation of cacti, twigs, and dying animals in the dry grass. Maybe the rugged limestone of the hillside will take them, swallow them whole, absorb bone into its belly as an offering. A plea. A prayer to guide her out of the clutches of the monster lurking in the Texas Hill Country.

Amber light pierces the tree line. The little bird squints, her eyes strain as they adjust against the dark. Fog roils down the hill with her as she nears a small home beyond the veil of the curtain of live oak.

She wants to scream, but her voice hitches. Why can't she scream? Copper. Grunting. Lightning. An overwhelming of the senses. Her mind dissociates and reminds her that she's not a wild animal. She's a *person*. She shouldn't have to cry out because *people aren't supposed to hunt other people.*

Little bird raps against the dusty screen door in sixteenth notes. Her fingers drag dirt and grime in small strokes of blood that splatter the vinyl siding. If she doesn't survive this then she will make her mark, *goddamnit.* Someone will know she was here.

A jaw harp twangs on the other side, plucking away against the teeth of someone inside. She yanks the handle, but the precarious latch inside the frame holds, remains locked, shuts her out. How can the person inside not hear her screaming so desperately for a lifeline?

Urgent and primal, she throws her head back and releases a guttural wail. Let the terrors of the night hear her. Let them come. Let them strip away whatever is left of her where she's standing. If she cannot break down the door with her hands, then she will do it with her voice.

The front door swings open. An elderly man points the barrel of a shotgun at her face. His finger hovers over the trigger, ready to blast her off his porch. His narrow eyes widen, soften, as recognition sweeps across his face.

"Michelle? Is that you?" Earl Skinner lowers his gun but remains on the other side of the screen door.

"Help me." Michelle rasps. "*Please.* He's coming!"

"What? Who's coming? You're bleeding everywhere. Are you hurt?"

"Open the door, Earl. Open the damn door!" A river of tears carves a path through mud and crusted blood down Michelle's cheeks. She slams the screen door against the frame again. How is it that she feels more flightless on the outside?

Earl shakes his head and unlocks the latch. Before Michelle can push her way inside, Earl steps forward putting himself between her and a wood paneled living room.

"Mr. Skinner, please! You don't understand. He's going to kill me!"

"Now just slow down. Who is going to kill you?" Earl grips the shotgun, the cross-bolt-trigger safety clip open and ready to fire.

Michelle's face goes numb. His name… *Goddamnit…* Why can't she remember the bastard's name? He was so familiar to her, but she couldn't place where she knew him from or why.

"Doesn't matter. No one comes on my property with intent to kill unless it's me. Which way do I go?"

"No, you can't! You don't understand—"

"I don't need to understand. I just need to aim and shoot." Earl steps off the porch and charges past mountain laurels into the twisted oak, letting the porch light dim behind him.

Another surge of pain travels down Michelle's leg in forte. Her eyes are fixed on the copse of trees, and they watch as the outline of Earl's figure joins the shadows there. Nerves shot, her heart rate spikes a tremolo as she runs into the heart of darkness.

A cold sweat breaks across her skin as luminescence frays. Michelle's vision darkens into a vignette, her periphery hazing over. She follows the sound of labored breathing. Is it ahead of her or behind her? She cannot discern which is Earl and which is the man with the scarred face who's name she cannot place. Wind whispers through cedar as a barn owl hoots.

This is his territory. Intruders are not allowed. Danger is near.

Michelle falls to her knees. She should have stayed at the house and waited for Earl to come back. His wife, Lizzy, is supposed to be a Christian prophetic woman. She could have helped Michelle. It doesn't matter now. Michelle is alone and bleeding out.

She closes her eyes and focuses on the Hill Country's lullaby. A chorus of crickets, the grunting of squirrels, croaking frogs, and the occasional groan of a deer. Even now, she can hear the faint sound of the jaw harp thrumming from the Skinner's home. A call to turn back before losing contact on the dark side of the moon.

A cough—wet, coagulated and phlegmy—interrupts her brief moment of peace, and a loud thud forces Michelle to open her eyes. Fatigued and dying, she cranes her neck anyway and sees Earl Skinner laying next to her. She reaches out to him, frantic to touch something human before life slips through her lips in a final breath. Earl shushes her and turns onto his back, his shotgun clutched against his chest.

Michelle just wanted to fly free. To soar from this place where dreams are abandoned, to abate the harsh batterings of reality. She holds the denim loop of Earl's waistband and holds her breath.

Twigs snap. Undergrowth crackles. The heavy grunts return. A sickening squelch followed by a paroxysm of rage—the glint of a blade sliding out of Michelle's chest cavity. The taste of pennies bubbles up her throat.

Michelle looks past her killer's face at the treetops swaying in the breeze, barely registering the blast of the shotgun next to them. How lovely it would be to touch the sky right now…to clutch moondust in her hands… to feel the heat of its ashen glow.

The jaw harp's song ceases. Michelle spreads her wings.

SHOOT OUT THE LIGHTS

THEY'LL BE PASSED *out by morning.*

A richness of swallows clad in black and white strut through The Teegarden Saloon. Chests puffed out with leather fringe fluttering against painted-on jeans, the bachelorette party looks like a group of nestlings barely old enough to buy their own drinks. Their dazzling smiles brim with anticipation of possibility. Nervous to lose a fleeting moment of youth, yet emboldened by the chance to make their mark. Their brand. They're hot as iron and they know it.

Darlene Boone watches from behind the bar like the white-tailed deer observing with careful silence, waiting for the kestrel to swoop in talons first. She envies their optimism. Do they know the danger hovering in their midst? The cost of their brazen naivety?

"Well, there's a sight for sore eyes." Ezra Klein tips his Stetson their way and winks.

"Aren't they a little young for you?" Orville Durham, ever cautious, comments.

"Just because they're off the menu don't mean I can't look none." Ezra's lips curl into a wry grin, turning him into a mischievous coyote much to the chagrin of the bachelorette party.

"Guess they don't want an old cowboy, after all," Randy Hoffmann says from the bottom of a pilsner glass. Ezra snorts and raises his drink to the girls anyway.

Darlene rolls her eyes as she dries a pint, kneading the washrag into the bottom of the glass in search of hidden smudges. Ezra, Orville, and Randy—men old enough to be her father—cluck like hens as they chatter on about the triumphs and struggles of the week. Their leathered skin, calloused hands, and sawdust cologne hold a lifetime of memories working alongside their fathers and grand-fathers. Even in September, there is no relief under the hot Texas sun. Mercy can only be found in the twilight, when the sun dips below the horizon and gives way to the cool blanket of night.

"What do you think Darlene?" Ezra asks, bringing Darlene back to Earth.

"Hmm?"

"About what happened to Earl Skinner."

"I reckon it ain't none of my business," she says. Madder than a wet hen, Darlene's stare cuts through the three of them. "And I imagine it's none of yours, neither."

"Aw hell, sure it is!" Randy says. "It happened not more than two miles from my orchard. If there's a killer on the loose, we ought to know so we can defend ourselves."

"And your precious peaches." Ezra teases.

Randy Hoffman waves his hand, shooing the comment away as he takes another swig. Hoffmann Orchards was a five-generation, family-owned operation since his second-great-grandfather immigrated to the middle-of-nowhere Texas in the 1800's. Like many German immigrants in the surrounding area, Randy's ancestors took to planting orchards, growing berries, and the likes. Peaches are what they were known for, though, and the Hoffmann family takes a great deal of pride in their legacy. Many of Randy's peers have already lost their family farms to rising operational costs, but Randy refuses to be the son who loses his family's orchard. No, he fully intends to pass down the operation to his daughter, a student at the University of Texas in Austin, earning her bachelor's degree in food and animal sciences.

"I tell you what," Randy begins, "I ain't never had the gumption to wander out into the sticks at night like that poor sumbitch. Something ain't right there."

"Earl never did have horse sense. The man's always been a little off his rocker, don't you reckon?" Ezra replies.

"Don't matter none what he was like. The man's guts were tore up like a wild hog got 'em, gored him right in the stomach." Orville cleans his glasses, then taps the bar top with his finger as a silent gesture to Darlene to go ahead and pour him another.

Darlene purses her lips and pours, pretends not to hear about the mess that's rattled the entire town these last forty-eight hours.

"The point being," Randy continues, "there's something out there, and we need to protect what's ours. It's our God-given right!"

"Ain't nobody coming after your damn peaches. Settle down. None of this land is ours, anyway. We're all just visitors trying to enjoy its beauty." Ezra looks down the bar at a young brunette. She's wearing a pink retro-Western top with red piping and hearts for buttons that practically screams she's a tourist. Her hair is set in curls, and her face is caked with makeup.

"It ain't real, Ezra," Orville says coolly. "I guarantee you that buckle-bunny is only here to find herself a rodeo star tonight. Doubtful she could find her way around the reins."

"Like I care," Ezra says as he waves her way. The young woman smiles and leans into her friend next to her, who is equally young and attractive. She's wearing a plaid work shirt and looks like she'd rather focus on the bottom of her glass than her friend making eyes at Ezra from across the bar. Buckle-bunnies or not, the pair were definitely here to experience The Teegarden, not to swap numbers with an old cowboy whose legacy in the arena was already long forgotten.

The Teegarden Saloon's famous reputation stems from its relationship with legendary country music singers of the past. Amid what looks like a shanty shack of timber and exposed knotty beams, signed portraits of icons like Patsy Cline, Glen Campbell, and Charley Pride hang proudly on the walls. Signed guitars, bold red leather boots, and old license plates on the wall shine proudly next to music memorabilia and a beloved taxidermized head of a Texas longhorn affectionately named Rusty. Anyone who was someone in the world of country music kicked off their careers at The Teegarden in one way or another, under the neon lights. Much like the famous cannon at the Alamo in San Antonio, visiting The Teegarden Saloon was a rite of passage for true fans of the scene. Be it devotees of rock-a-billy, Honky-tonk, the smooth "Nashville Sound," or folks itching for a taste of Louisiana Zydeco, all were welcome through The Teegarden's doors.

"How are you holding up, sweetie?" Orville's voice drops low. "You doing okay round the bend?"

Darlene was fortunate to live on a small homestead her grandfather's grandfather earmarked to live and work on when he moved to Texas. It was a small woodcutter's cottage, made from limestone and mesquite, that provided enough necessities and small comforts to call home. To Darlene, it was one part time capsule, two parts safe haven.

"Never been better." She smirks, pours Orville a shot of whiskey on the house. "That piece of shit is still dead, ain't he?" The piece of shit she is referring to is Leroy, her husband— *dead* husband.

Uglier than homemade sin, Leroy was a drunk, a cheater, a liar, and a wife beater. Everyone in town knew as much. Women whispered about Darlene's predicament in church and men eyed Leroy suspiciously whenever they saw him staggering, drunk, around town, but for the most part, everyone kept their concerns to themselves. "Minded their own," as folks would say. And now, in the case of Earl, Darlene was saying the same.

The only locals to ever stand up for Darlene were Randy, Ezra, and Orville. On more than one occasion— at The Teegarden, no less—one of the three had squared up with Leroy. They, too, had their suspicions, but they couldn't call him out on them without Darlene suffering the consequences, so instead they picked fights with Leroy over minor squabbles, like an unpaid tab or a spilled drink. Leroy, in return, usually beat the snot out of them.

It was only after Leroy died in a house fire that Darlene was finally rid of him.

"Oh, I know. That sumbitch is rotting in hell for what he did to you, but dead snakes can still bite. Like that handsy feller here the other day, wouldn't leave you alone. Whatever happened to him?

Darlene flashes her hand, rings on each finger. "I gave him a five-knuckle goodbye. Gave it to him pretty good, too, if I do say so myself. Opa taught me how to throw a mean hook growing up. Left a nasty gash across his face for it."

It was true; Darlene beat the shit out of that straggler. Drunk as a skunk, the man followed her to her car, searching for action. When she refused him, he got physical. He grabbed Darlene's wrist and pinned her to her truck, a little tan Chevy S-10 2000 in need of a paint job real bad. But instead of panicking, she kneed him in the crotch and socked him in the left orbital bone so hard he bled. She then jumped in her truck and sped away, watched him drop to one knee in her rearview mirror. With any luck, he'd offer himself up as buzzard bait, but she knew his type, knew better than to hope. He'd be back. Wounded pride was a powerful motivator for evil men.

"Well, if you ever need it, you just give a holler and we'll be right there." Randy tips the brim of his hat toward her. "Lord knows if my little girl finds herself a husband, or any man for that matter, and he wallops on her, I'd make damn sure they'd never be found at the bottom of that sinkhole."

"Thanks, Randy." *But it shouldn't be because you have a daughter.* Darlene acts amiable anyway and reminds herself she has all three men's phone numbers saved in her cell phone. Not that it matters much tonight. She left her phone at home, and cell phone service is useless at The Teegarden anyway. The bar relies on a single landline to connect to the outside world. Wanda, the owner, says it's part of The Teegarden's charm. *"Step back in time, sit a spell, and forget your troubles, Wi-Fi free!"*

"Hey sugar, are you rationed?" Ezra has found his way to the end of the bar to work his charm on the young brunette. She tucks her hair behind her ear and bats her lashes. Her friend rolls her eyes and gives Darlene a knowing look, like this is a common occurrence for them. Darlene wants to tell her that it's common for Ezra, too, but instead throws a washrag over her shoulder and grabs a serving tray to bring the next round of drinks.

"Watch the register, will you?" She throws Randy and Orville a wink as she rounds the bar. A couple Shiner Bocks, a Karbach IPA, a double shot of whiskey neat, and vodka-cranberries for the bachelorette party.

"When's the live music starting? We came here for a show!" a voice shrills somewhere from the amalgamation of women.

"I want to hear Beyoncé!"

"The night's still young, ladies. Next round is on that man over there." Darlene points to Ezra, who nods their way.

"WOOOOO!" the universal cry of the bachelorette party released, notoriety held at bay.

"Where y'all from?" Darlene asks as she passes out drinks.

"Tuscon," the bride says. "We're staying about fifteen minutes down the road in an Airbnb."

"We went on a wine tour. It was so fun!" another chirps as she toe taps rhinestone boots to the beat of the jukebox music.

"Did y'all take a photo in front of the sign?" A staple of the property, The Teegarden's blazing neon sign and string lights connected the bar to an outdoor dance hall for its summer concert series and gift shop. Both are dark tonight on account of the bad weather rolling through.

"Oh my God, yes! But there's no service out here, so I couldn't post it online." The bride pouts as her lip gloss reflects ribbons of light above them.

"That's kind of the point," Darlene chides.

Where the hell were the musicians? They should have been here twenty minutes ago. Darlene can't think of anything worse than a bratty bachelorette party not getting their way.

Like the flick of a pick on a guitar riff, Darlene two-steps over to the jukebox to change songs. With arms wide and outstretched, she sways to the music, knowing full well some of the customers are thinking of what it would be like to two-step alongside her; how it would feel to grip her hips to a slow dance as ballads belt through the speaker. A tight pair of Wranglers will put just about anyone under its spell, especially on a buxom blonde with curves made for riding.

Darlene lets them dream on and dares to bat her baby blues at a few of the non-regulars who decided to come in tonight. They know they can't have her but will leave hefty tips anyway.

Call it liberation or subjugation, Darlene doesn't care. She just knows that there's power in wielding desire.

ULTRAVIOLET

A CURRENT OF whiskey flows from amber bottles down to soft leather boots keeping tempo with the music playing in the speakers. Lovers grasp each other's hands, genteel with understanding, as the ballad sweeps them across the floor. Slow, steady, and wanton with a desire that eddies like the haze of a heat wave, they dance like binary stars inextricably bound together.

"You got that look again, Wildflower." Wanda Higgins gives Darlene a knowing smile as she taps her cherry-red acrylic nails against her glass, waiting for acknowledgment. Darlene doesn't notice and continues to watch the couples glide, their steps blurring into a dust cloud of solar wind.

"Houston to Darlene, come-in!"

"Sorry—what were you saying?"

"I said you got that look again."

"What look?"

"Like you're some space cadet lost in the stars. Anywhere but here." Wanda arches her brow, a dark brown that stands out in contrast to the cool salt and pepper strands of her hair. With every passing year she wears her aging beauty with grace, refusing to be sidelined as a woman in her sixties. Not only is Wanda the sole owner of The Teegarden (forty years and counting), she is also Darlene's predecessor as the long-time bartender here and the closest thing Darlene has to family.

Darlene cracks a smile that doesn't meet her eyes. She shakes her head as she preps a vodka-cranberry for Wanda.

"So, who are you all dolled up for tonight?" Darlene says, changing the subject.

"Is it that obvious?" Wanda rolls her eyes. "Some guy named Luis, though I haven't met him before. One of the ladies at church set me up with the fella, saying he was a tall glass of water that used to drive trucks. So, he must be settled down and enjoying retirement at this point." Wanda gives Darlene a playful poke. "You'd know if you showed up to mass once in a while."

"I'm not sitting next to folks who'd never deign to break bread with me. Not sure why you would either."

"Not even for a good bit of gossip?" Wanda smirks and takes a sip of her drink before catching her reflection in the gold leaf mirror behind the bar. She touches her hair—gently tousled feather bangs and voluminous curls—and admires the woman staring back at her in the mirror. Hidden behind memory lines and crow's feet is a glimmer of the young woman Wanda used to be.

"My stars… I look like a young Farrah Fawcett with this hairstyle, don't I? Like a real *Charlie's Angel.*" She lets out a chuckle before worry lines etch her face. "This is silly, isn't it? Does it look like I'm trying too hard? Should I cancel?"

"I think," Darlene says as she brushes a fly-away from Wanda's face, "you look fantastic and deserve a night out. You never do anything for yourself."

"Because I don't need to. I'm too busy looking after you and"—she gestures to Ezra making a fool of himself at the

end of the bar before nodding to Randy and Orville—
"this lot here. You're all I've got."

"No one asked you to be our mother hen, Wanda."
Randy teases.

"Well, someone's got to look after the roost."

As Wanda continues to play with her hair in the mirror,
a large gray mass obstructs her view.

"*Jesus of Nazareth!* I know you did not bring that
varmint in here, Darlene!"

Darlene turns around to greet Levi, her pet opossum.
The animal is perched atop the barback with the liquor
bottles and tchotkes, oblivious to the way he is blocking
Wanda's reflection. Tonight he's wearing a little cowboy
hat, something Darlene picked up at a pet boutique in
town. It was probably for a small dog, but it fit Levi just
fine, and he didn't seem to mind. Levi yawns, then displays
a toothy grin before nuzzling Darlene's arm for a pet. She
obliges, carefully scooping him up in her arms.

"Oh, he's not hurting anyone by being here, Wanda. You
know as well as I he's nothing but a sleepy paperweight.
Besides, everyone loves him. Ain't no one gonna snitch
to the health department." She nods to the bachelorette
party cooing and making baby noises at Levi.

"Just keep him under the bar, will you? You might
think they won't snitch, but you never truly know with
strangers."

With her boot, Darlene scooches a feathered dog bed
out from beneath the bar and picks it up, one-handed.
She then places it atop a relic from the 1950s—an old
cooler with a classic Miller High Life logo and red paint
that's slowly rusted away. The cooler is out of sight for
most patrons, as per Wanda's request, but this way, Levi
can spy the locals as they belly up to the bar, hoping for
a treat. All the regulars at The Teegarden know he likes

leftover McDonald's french fries and Jack Link's beef jerky, and they come prepared. Darlene sets Levi down in his bed, then turns to Wanda for approval, who just shakes her head and promptly reaches for a small bottle of hand sanitizer in her purse.

"Think you might settle down? Retire?" Randy asks Wanda.

"Oh, no. I don't think I could ever completely retire. I mean, what would I do all day? Sit on my porch drinking sun tea like the rest of these heifers? Watch tumbleweed blow in the breeze? Pff." Wanda's glass thuds quietly on the knotty bar top as she thinks briefly on the notion of life without the bar. "I suppose I could join one of those groups and become an activist. Could you imagine me, little ol' Wanda, at the front of a picket line?"

"Yes," Randy and Orville say in unison.

"You've done it before," Darlene chimes in, reminding Wanda of her days as a flower child marching through the streets of Austin, then later as the young wife of a steelworker on the Gulf Coast before moving back to the Hill Country, where she and her husband Henry met and befriended Darlene's grandparents.

"Screaming and hollering at the big boss is a young person's game, and I don't have that sort of fighting spirit left in me darlin'. But I tell you what," she says, her bony index finger wagging at nothing in particular, "if I do retire in any capacity, I'm leaving The Teegarden to you."

"You are not." Darlene scoffs. "That's the liquor talking."

"Oh, yes I am!" She meets Darlene's gaze, vodka-cranberry in hand. "Who else would I leave it to? Don't have any children of my own. And Lord knows I'm not leaving this place to that fool nephew of mine. All he's good for is landing himself in prison." She rubs the polished wood of the bar top, glassy-eyed. "My daddy started this place from nothing. I can't let it fall into the hands of one of those corporate weenies. They'd ruin it with franchises, take it national, and take the magic with it. It needs to stay local, with you."

"Wanda, I don't want you thinking I expect something from you."

"I know you don't, hon.'"

"I mean it. You're one of the few friends I have in this town. You're important to me." Darlene finds her hand in Wanda's own. She is the person Darlene trusts the most, the keeper of her fears and secrets. Wanda cups Darlene's cheek and grimaces as she fights back the tears welling in her eyes.

"You've been through a lot, Wildflower. Now, I know you like your job here just fine. Hell, I liked it too when I served here in my youth—"

"So did we!" Randy grunts. Wanda swats his shoulder and continues.

"But one day you'll be tired of serving drinks to old men talking a heap of nonsense each night when they should be home with their wives. You need a long-term plan, and I trust you can take care of the saloon when I'm gone. You can run the business, even hire a few more bartenders. You know the heart that keeps this place beating. Know its *soul*. You deserve this."

"I don't want to do that *now*—serving beer to old men, I mean."

"Well, now I'm offended," says Orville. He clutches his chest, feigning insult.

Wanda waves off the sentiment. "If you have to, think of it as a part of your inheritance. Your grandmother was a dear friend of mine." She points to an acrylic painting of The Teegarden saloon hanging on the wall between a horseshoe and a signed photo of

Willie Nelson. Darlene's grandmother had painted it. "She was such a gift, such a light in my life. It's only right. Besides, we need more women running this town these days. Gotta remind the menfolk that we, too, are a force to be reckoned with."

"Don't I know it," Randy chuffs as he sips his beer.

"Besides the old guys," Darlene laughs, "I like it here."

"You like security, Darlene." Wanda crosses her arms and side-eyes Darlene. "It's been a year since—well, you know. Isn't it time you challenge yourself? I'll let you shadow me a couple nights a week to get the hang of running the books."

"I don't know, Wanda—"

"And while we're at it, isn't it about time you stepped out on your own, too? You're too young and too beautiful to let your good looks wither away behind this bar. You should be out there, causin' a little ruckus."

"Who says I don't cause a little ruckus?"

"Bless your heart if you call *one* rendezvous with a stranger you met at a bar 'causing ruckus.' Back when I first started serving here, I was breaking more than a few hearts."

"You can say that again," Orville says before taking a sip. The comment sounds more bitter than he means it to, and Wanda shoots a look at him.

Darlene knows where the conversation is headed, but she's not ready to have it. A year isn't enough time to mend a heart that's been trampled on. And it's not like she didn't try. It's just hard to strip down and bare oneself when your body was once covered in bruises. She sees them still, sometimes, those painful reminders that Leroy still haunts her. Wanda means well, but all her prodding does is make Darlene want a cigarette.

"Can I take my break? I'll be back in five minutes."

A deflated Wanda agrees, and scoots cautiously past Levi, careful not to touch him as she takes her place behind the bar—if he so much as hisses at her, she'll jump out of her britches. Muscle memory returns to her, and within the wag of an opossum's tail, she's pouring out a cold one at one of the high tops and handing it to a pleased customer. If it were anyone other than Wanda, the regulars would have a fit.

THE NIGHT IS arid and warm on Darlene's skin, a reprieve from the humid September day in the Hill Country. The old *Farmer's Almanac* thermometer nailed to the side of The Teegarden reads eighty degrees Fahrenheit, just cool enough to enjoy a gentle breeze swaying between the scraggly oak trees, their limbs reaching skyward toward the stars.

Even in the twilight—that hedge between two different worlds, where blue bleeds into gold—Darlene can barely make out the thick band of the Milky Way. She wonders how it could be that so many stars in the sky were actually dead, their present light an echo, a memory, from millions of years in the past. Stars were kind of like the Wild West heroes of old, she thought. Strong, stoic, burning bright and dying in a blaze of glory out on the open range, free of life's mundanities. Their legacies, oftentimes, unheralded until centuries later, when their impact was felt most. Legacies modern cowboys could only dream of emulating, many of whom were stuck in the chute on the back of a bull, caught up in the glamour of small-town stardom, dangerous with the possibility that none of this is real, or worse—that this is as good as it will ever get.

The crunch of gravel shifts Darlene's attention toward the outdoor dance hall. She stills like the white-tailed deer again, stopping to listen for a coyote creeping round the bend. Crickets croak, bat wings flutter. Darlene jumps back, startled, as one of the hidden bats streaks suddenly across her vision, darting left and right through the velvet night. Up ahead, a human silhouette appears and starts to come near.

"Hello?" a woman's voice calls out. "Hello? Can we get some help over here?"

Darlene's eyes narrow as she puts out her cigarette in the ashtray stand on the porch. A ringtail hops between the barbs of cacti growing next to the wood-plank steps at her feet and lowers its snout to glean food between the leaves and twigs on the ground.

"Come into the light!" Darlene says. She rolls back her shoulders to stand just a bit taller, projecting an exaggerated show of strength for the stranger.

"Ugh, fine."

The sound of squeaky wheels being dragged slowly across the gravel drive ends when a rickety dolly loaded with boxes is illuminated by the neon glow of The Teegarden's sign. A tall woman, with strawberry hair and a folk-style dress, is at the dolly's helm, and she's struggling something fierce to drag it forward for Darlene to see.

"It's just really heavy, and my boyfriend is back at the van unloading the rest of our equipment. We didn't realize it would be such a hike from the parking lot."

"Oh," says Darlene, lowering her guard. She can see now that the woman is part of tonight's musical act, the one the bachelorette party has been waiting for. "You're with the band. Thought maybe you were just some hitchhiker in trouble."

The woman parks her dolly next to the porch before leaning on one of the pillars to catch her breath. "Sorry if I scared you. We've never played at this venue before and got a little lost finding our way through the back roads. It gets so dark out here. We had to follow the fence posts just to stay on the road."

"Well, you're here now. What can I help you with?"

FROM CAN TO CAIN'T

LAMBENT BEAMS BATHE Hazel's waxen face, the rainbow of string lights melting together in purple haze. Muffled crackles from the amplifier remind her of the grackles she heard outside her hotel window earlier this morning in San Antonio. A deafening swarm of chatter that stirred her from slumber in the cockcrow hour.

"You sound off. Try again," Tim says, his face a stone slab.

"Maybe it's the tuner? Can you adjust it?" she asks.

"It's not me. I'm telling you it's you."

Hazel belts out a couple of notes, looking to Tim for approval. He shakes his head. Hazel slumps, takes a sip of water, and lets out a heavy sigh.

"Looks like you both could use a stiff drink," says Darlene. "The drive out here has a way of tensing the nerves if one's not familiar with the roads." She hands the two of them a double shot of bourbon.

"You can say that again," Tim replies before swallowing the double shot in one gulp.

Hazel sips the bourbon and scrunches up her face, disgusted. "What he means to say is that we're just not accustomed to so many winding roads. We're from the low country in South Carolina. This is the farthest west we've ever been."

"Ain't got no hills in those parts?"

"If you count flat roads and sandy soil, then sure, we've got hills," Hazel quips, finishing the rest of her drink.

Cross-armed, the pouting bachelorette party glowers at the three of them from across the room. Their drinks are watered down, in need of a refill of something stronger than vodka-cranberries to temper their growing impatience.

"Y'all ready to play?" Darlene asks. "The bachelorette over there is gettin' restless."

Tim strums a G-chord on his guitar. It's perfectly in tune. "We're ready," he says.

Darlene nods and turns toward the sound tech next to the bar, gives him the thumbs up to dim the lights and cut the jukebox feed.

The overhead lights go off, the stage lights come on, and the jukebox music cuts out. All that remains is the clinking of glasses and the raucous din of the crowd.

Hazel and Tim start to play.

After just one song, Darlene understands why Wanda booked them. When Darlene closes her eyes, she pictures herself at the Grand Ole Opry, listening to some younger version of Parton, Lynn, or Wynette. And when she opens them, she sees a honky-tonk angel up there on that stage, her aura glowing red, white, and blue. Tim, meanwhile, sits in stoic fashion behind Hazel, effortlessly strumming the melodies on his guitar in subdued, workmanlike fashion. He knows it's Hazel and not him who's the real star of this show, and he's okay with that so long as he gets to play.

Ezra finds his way to the dance floor with the brunette he's been sweet-talkin', whom Darlene learns is named

Brandy. She's never understood how Ezra charms his much younger paramours into a night of debauchery and reckless loving, but here he is, doing it again. Brandy toys with his hat, a dusty cattleman-style with a pinched front, until she places it upon her own head. Ezra's Cheshire grin says all that needs to be said in the space between him and his friends—the man's as good as gone for the night, and she's coming with him.

Darlene isn't paying attention to Ezra, though. She's got her eye on a suspicious shadow lurking outside one of the dance hall windows. It appears to be a man, and though she can't see his face, she also can't shake the feeling that he's looking directly at her.

"Randy," Darlene starts. "Do you see that man?"

Randy looks up from his drink and raises his voice just loud enough to be heard over Hazel's twangier, more aggressive cover of Shania Twain's "You're Still the One."

"Darlin', I have no interest in watching that dipshit make a fool of himself with a woman half his age."

"Not Ezra; the one over there, in the window." She points. "Do you see him?"

Randy swivels his stool and looks in the general direction her finger has hexed. He squints, then nods. "Probably finishing a cig. Why? You worried?"

"Maybe. I don't know. It just feels a little creepy, I guess, to be staring through the window like that. Most folks take their smokes by the door."

"Think he's playing with his pecker?" Orville asks.

"Gross," Darlene says, embarrassed by the thought.

"Fine." Randy grunts. "I'll go check it out. Can't have fellers playing with their peckers outside the bar. It's bad for business." He winks at Darlene then slaps Orville on the back. "Watch my beer."

"Yes, dear," Orville agrees.

After Randy exits, Wanda takes his seat. She fishes a compact from her purse and holds the mirror out in front of her so she can give her lipstick a final check. "They're good, right?" she asks, nodding backward at the band while still inspecting herself in the mirror.

"Better than I expected," Darlene answers.

Wanda licks her teeth and snaps the mirror closed. "I do know how to pick 'em," she says with a smile.

Orville eyes the cherry-red lipstick on Wanda's lips. "Big date tonight?"

"Yes, sir," she replies.

"Hope the feller knows who he's dealing with."

Wanda puts an elbow on the bar top and leans over just far enough to stare daggers into Orville's eyes. "And what's that supposed to mean?"

"It means you get bored easily, have a temper, and can start an argument with an empty house."

Wanda takes her weight off her elbow and slaps the bar top with her hand. "Well, damn, Orville! Tell me how you really feel."

"I just did!"

"All right, love birds, settle down now," Darlene intervenes. "It's hotter than Satan's pits in here, and I don't have the patience for squabbling."

FOX HOLE

THE WOODRAT STANDS in the open, in search of what or whom he does not know. Lured outside the safety of its den, the scent of vanilla and oak carries on a breeze. He does not see the gray fox who hungers for his bones, does not know it is ready to pounce on him, sever his spinal cord, and savor the taste of his suffering.

Outside, Randy treads carefully, drawn to the shapely figure of a woman leaning against the outdoor dance floor's outermost column. He's cautious to approach the present the fox has left him; he knows something isn't right, but he can't look away. His lips tremble, and his face goes numb at the sight. Dried blood smatters the woman's pant leg and chest, and whatever is left of her shirt is tattered and folded into the mutilated flesh of her chest cavity. Her face is concealed behind a mess of matted hair clumped with ryegrass and twigs.

"Ma'am?" he whispers. "Ma'am, can you hear me?"

He knows she can't but asks anyway. The woman does not reply. Every instinct in Randy's body screams for him to run, go back to the safety of the bar, but he's never been one to turn away from the face of danger, never one to avoid risk. He's the kind of man who stares down the gaping maw of his own destruction, and he can feel that destruction approach. Once he's close enough to the woman, he can tell she's most likely dead. There's also something strangely familiar about her. A horrible feeling wrenches his stomach as he peels back the curtain of hair from her face.

The woman is his daughter, Michelle.

Her eyes—those beautiful hazel eyes Randy used to marvel at—have been plucked clean from their sockets, and all that remains are two gaping holes, the flesh there tattered and bloody, as if picked at by wild birds or animals. Her face is bruised and bloated, a bloody dell of gobbets and viscera, a swollen slurry of black and red.

The sound that escapes his throat is primal, a cry that claws the sky with rage. The gray fox is pleased. *Good.* He wants this. He revels in witnessing his adversary's horror, their grief, their spiraling descent into madness. It makes their eventual death all the more satisfying. Adrenaline may spoil the meat, but the anticipation of his kill heightens the experience.

Randy turns toward the inescapable nothingness that swells in the pockets of trees. It seeps, stringy strands of cedar bleeding from bark. Can anyone in The Teegarden hear his cries over the roar of music that plays inside? Can they hear his world unraveling? He feels suspended in time, watching everyone else carry on without him.

Randy barrels through the dark, a stocky javelina, wiry and thrashing. He sweeps the area, lumbering toward the only thing that makes sense in this sudden hell. Just beyond the stage of the outdoor dance hall, a man stands at the ready with a pitchfork pointed squarely at Randy's chest.

Randy grunts before charging who he can only assume is his daughter's killer. He's reaching for his .22, but he doesn't realize the safety is off. He's too focused on the righteous violence he is going to bring down upon this man, upon this right hand of the devil, and the Godly vengeance he will soon extract for the five-year-old girl with the gap-toothed grin who grew up to be just another woman slaughtered on the open road.

But before he can draw the pistol, the gun goes off in its holster and blows a dime-sized hole into Randy's thigh, causing him to scream out in pain and tumble sideways. He falls into a nearby column and grabs it for stability, claws at it in a painful effort to stay on his feet. He knows that if he falls, he's dead.

Randy's lungs burn, every breath feels like wildfire, and his panicked gasps serve only to quicken the blood loss from his wound. By the looks of it, the femoral artery is damaged. The surrounding flesh feels warm and wet, but it's not until he falls to his knees that the bite of the bullet truly stings.

Guilt tightens around Randy's neck like a noose. He should have known Michelle was in trouble; he should have been there to protect his baby girl. Maybe if he taught her how to hold a gun, how to aim and fire, like his father had taught Randy growing up, she'd have been able to defend herself. Randy never wanted Michelle to fight for her life, to know the struggle of survival. Michelle was different, better than Randy would ever be. Visions flood his mind's eye: two-year-old Michelle toddling into the kitchen for a hug from daddy; twiggy, eight-year-old Michelle on her first fishing trip; seventeen-year-old Michelle lost in the pageantry of the uniquely Texas tradition of wearing an oversized homecoming mum, its blue and white ribbons reminding

Randy of a prize-winning mare at the county fair before biting his tongue. Her life stolen in an instant. Randy watches the shadow-man saunter toward him, lazily dragging the pitchfork across the concrete foundation. The scrape of metal is an assault on Randy's senses, and he winces.

"*You*—" Randy chokes. He can't get the words out of his mouth. Every fiber of his being tells him to get up and run, *crawl* if that's all he can muster, but he can't bring himself to budge.

The rusty prongs of the pitchfork puncture Randy's abdomen with ease. They slide smoothly inside like he's a scarecrow made of hay. The pain is blinding, sharp, and it emanates deep from within Randy's bowels. Blood spurts onto his chest in response.

"What…," Randy wheezes, "do you…want?" His vision struggles like a cloudy vignette on an old tintype photograph. His attacker's face is barely visible, a whisper in the dark that eddies with ribbons of scarred flesh and malice beneath the neon lights. The stranger leans in close, his fiery breath against Randy's ear.

"I want justice. I want your suffering. I want to watch the light leave your eyes as I pulverize you on the end of this stick." The man then rips the prongs from Randy's body, and watches with grim delight as more blood pours from the freshly opened wounds.

Randy studies everything he can about the man standing over him just in case he makes it out of this predicament alive: *bald, scar over the left eye; keloids on his cheeks and scalp;the urge to kill chiseled into his deformed face.* He refuses to look away.

Death hovers over Randy like the rain clouds stirring above. Sensing the end is near, he shouts one final curse at the man before his voice is silenced forever by the pitchfork being stabbed into his throat. The man places his boot against Randy's shoulder for leverage and yanks the pitchfork free. And though what's left of Randy's legacy bleeds out onto the concrete, the killer is not yet done. The man stabs him again and again and again, puncturing every organ, cracking every rib, pulverizing every ounce of flesh until it's nothing more than pulp. Randy's head lolls to the side, his eyes fixated on Michelle's corpse.

I'm sorry, baby girl. I'm so sorry.

The pits of Michelle's eyes swallow him whole.

MOONLIGHT KISSES

FAT RAINDROPS PITTER patter against the metal roof like the clatter of spoons on tin cans. In the distance, a lightning strike decimates a lone tree, charring it black. Thunder rumbles, and a draft wafts in through an open window, carrying with it the petrichor of rain. The air grows heavy and wet with a humidity that's thick like ichor, and Darlene knows they're in for something strong this evening.

Levi hisses from his bed, the wiry hairs on his back raised in alert. He hates storms. Darlene scratches the soft skin behind his ear to reassure him, but he's staring at her with those beady eyes like he doesn't believe her.

"Relax, little boy. It ain't nothing to worry about."

Being left with no other choice, Levi returns to chewing on the fruit salad Darlene had packed for him this afternoon. He pops another grape in his mouth with his teeth.

The bachelorette party must be feeling the alcohol now, because they're all looking for moonlight kisses from unsuspecting strangers, and a few even throw seductive winks at tired cowboys who quite obviously just want to be left alone They're content enough mulling over their bourbons and nodding along to Hazel's soulful country crooning, the same way they nod their heads when listening to the local pastor preach.

Darlene locks eyes with one of the men. He's suntanned, with dark eyes and a jawline so sharp it might as well be a crime. Her cheeks flush. He's the one-night stand she had less than a month ago, and she realizes now that she never asked for his name. Not at the bar, not in her truck, not in his bed, and not the following morning as she slipped into her jeans before sunrise and left without a word. She didn't mean to stay over. Didn't want to get personal. Vulnerable.

She shifts her focus to Wanda, who is standing at a high-top, stirring her vodka-cranberry. The man next to her is her date, Luis, and by the look of it, Wanda's feigning interest in their conversation. She's bored, Darlene can tell. Probably had more fun watching paint dry. She makes her way over to where they're seated.

"How's it going? Can I refill your drinks?" she asks, collecting their empty glasses.

Wanda's eyes narrow, saying all that needs to be said with that one look. *I know what you're doing, Darlene Boone.*

"Oh, no," Wanda chuckles. "I don't think that'll be necessary."

Luis's face softens, and he clutches the brim of his hat. He's not sure what to say and swallows the lump in his throat. The sentiment in his eyes catches Wanda by surprise.

"I'm sorry. My momma raised me with better manners than that." Her voice is apologetic, but still firm in its conviction. "What I should have said is that I'm not ready to be back in the dating world. I realized that tonight. It's just all a bit much for me." She gestures to her hair and makeup. "This getup isn't me. Never has been. Truth is, I built my life with a man I'd known since I was eighteen years old, and now that he's gone, I'm lost. He took a part of me with him, and I'm struggling with how to replace it. You understand, Luis? I gotta figure out who I am without him; not who I can be for another man."

Luis nods. "I felt the same way after my wife Rita passed. We met in San Antonio, raised our family there, but she actually grew up here. In fact, she spent a lot of her youth in this very bar. Always talked highly of this place and all the good memories she made."

Darlene wonders if she and this man's late wife ever met. "You said her name was Rita?"

"Yes ma'am. Rita Ramírez—er, Rita Hammons at the time. She's been gone for three years, but it still feels like yesterday."

Realization sweeps across Wanda's face. "Rita Hammons?! I went to grade school with Rita Hammons! Her folks lived just down the road from mine in a little white farmhouse. Oh, I just loved visiting their farm as a child. I'd help feed their chickens." She laughs and shakes her head in pleasant disbelief. "What a small world," she muses.

"Tiny," Luis says with a smile.

"Oh hell, Luis. There's more to you in there, after all. Isn't there? And here I was thinking I was talking to a feller who didn't know how to carry on a conversation with a lady."

The melancholic hum of the dobro guitar in Tim's hands lulls the crowd into a slow dance. Those still seated sway in chairs.

Wanda ponders things for a moment. She might not be ready to date, but that doesn't mean she can't still enjoy the evening with a friend. And if Luis was good enough for Rita, then…

"Forgive me for being so forward," she says to Luis, "but may I have this dance? I just love this song, and a little two-step might be just what the doctor ordered to help pull us out of our doldrums."

Luis smiles and offers his hand. "It would be my pleasure, Miss Wanda."

Darlene winks at Wanda, but Wanda just rolls her eyes in response. She then turns to Luis, takes the man's hand, and strolls with him onto the dance floor.

As Darlene watches the couple take their first awkward dance steps together, a pang of sadness hits. The 'firsts' of any budding relationship are magical, a dizzying dream to be lost within. Darlene had that with Leroy once, or at least she thought she did.

It's times like these when things get lonely behind the bar. Maybe one day romance will find her again, but if it does, she won't be so quick to let herself fall. Betrayal soured her ability to trust her heart with anyone else, and how could she give herself to another when the last man she trusted shattered her the way he did? How could she ever look lovingly into another man's eyes again when all she ever saw was him?

ONE YEAR AGO

ROTGUT

A RED IMPRINT from the carpet fibers mars Darlene's face as she lifts her head off the living room floor. Dusk has descended, and the only light in the room is from the glow of television static emanating from the old Zenith laying on its side. She doesn't know what time it is; she must have been out for hours. Her temple throbs, and a wave of nausea overcomes her as she sits upright. It doesn't help that the room smells like Captain Morgan. Darlene hates the smell of rum and coke more than anything. It's Leroy's favorite drink.

The dark doesn't show her what she already knows because she can smell it. The blood seeps from the gash in her head. The rhythm of her heart quickens. Maybe she should lay back down and wait for a sign Leroy's fallen asleep.

The clang of silverware from the kitchen tells her otherwise. He's muttering to himself, stumbling into cabinets, rummaging through drawers, undoubtedly looking for the bottle opener Darlene threw away that morning. His breath is ragged, and heavy heaves punch the air like his knuckles on her face. She remembers now how she ended up on the floor: Leroy had shoved her, and she cracked her head against the coffee table on the way down. She's thankful she never purchased that glass-top table she saw at the Big Lots a few months back.

He is there, and she is here, alone, in the dark. Darlene slows her breathing to the point she can no longer hear her own breath. Like a lizard in the brush, she braces her weight on her hands and knees to crawl across the floor. Forget the go-bag. Leroy knows her plans to leave him, and he'll stop her the moment he sees her grab it. She needs to get out of this house and drive away; never look back. *But what about the car keys?* Leroy probably took those, too.

Shit.

Darlene could make a run for it. She knows the footpaths between the nearby orchards and ranches better than Leroy ever did. Unlike him, she grew up in these parts and spent her childhood being mindful of the rattlesnakes in the tall grass. She could find her way to a trusted neighbor's house, but those were few and far between, and the blanket of night brought other dangers. And if an animal feels caged, pushed back into a corner, it will swipe. It *will* bite. Could Darlene do that for herself? Could she fight for her survival if the moment demanded it?

A tug on her skirt hoists her up. Leroy yanks her collar and pulls Darlene backward onto her knees. His hands fist her hair, his knuckles digging into her skull. Back when they first met beneath the neon glow of The Teegarden, he'd told Darlene that her blonde curls were prettier than a field of sunflowers. Cheap words, Darlene knew, but they were good enough to open a door to her heart and home.

"I thought I told you to stay down, bitch." The words come out like a rabid dog frothing at the mouth. His hand moves to her neck, gripping until her face turns red, desperate for air. He lets go and tugs at her hair again.

"Fuck you!" She spits. She grabs his wrists and digs her nails into his skin. Leroy hisses, but he doesn't let go. Instead, he drags her into the hallway.

Darlene writhes under his grip. Her voice is raw from screaming and her scalp is on fire; the hair in her head feels like it's about to be ripped clean off. She's holding onto her hair now, trying to stop him from pulling her farther, but she can't get any traction. Her heels scuff the thin pine boards beneath her feet. She lets out a defeated whimper as Leroy drags her to their bedroom.

Wood panel walls, once warm and inviting, surround her like a fiberboard coffin illuminated by a standalone lamp in the corner. The green carpet is infused with the essence of old cigarettes, dirty nail clippings, and spilled beer. This room is suddenly unfamiliar and hostile. She looks out the window at the empty dirt road and the barbed wire fence that surrounds the property. The nearest neighbor is two miles away. Not a soul will hear her cries for help. She might as well be on the moon.

She imagines dead vines penetrate the electrical sockets and wood trim, cave the roof in so she can blast off to the stars. Everywhere she looks there's a nail on the wall and a ring of dust where photographs used to hang, erasing her from this place like tobacco stains on wallpaper.

Leroy releases her hair and drops Darlene to the floor. Before she can get her footing, he presses the palm of his hand into her face, pinning her to the ground with his body. He strokes his thumb against her jaw.

"We could have had it all, Sunflower." His lips graze her cheek as he moves his hand to the soft space of her belly. She recoils at his touch, doesn't want his hands on a part of her that is so vulnerable and intimate. She's thrashing and shrieking like a bobcat when a scream catches in her throat. Her lips curl. She clenches her teeth. Leroy pulls her up to her knees, and she sees now where their bed has been flipped over onto its side. Leroy must have found the extra cash she kept hidden for safekeeping.

"Let me go!"

"Oh no, you're not going anywhere." He shoves Darlene into the tiny closet. Her body hits the keepsake boxes stored on the floor with a thud. She tries to turn the loose knob with all her strength, but Leroy's already propped a chair beneath the knob on the other side, preventing her from wriggling the door open.

"Leroy! Leroy, let me out of here!" Darlene slams her body into the closet door with all her might. She scratches the wood slats, leaving indentations in the paint. Her middle finger splinters and bleeds.

"Leroy, please!" She pounds her fists on the door.

"What am I supposed to do when all you do is threaten to leave?" Words slurred, the whiskey hot on Leroy's breath like roadkill rotting in the sun. He unzips her go-bag and starts ransacking the contents. Clothes and keepsakes are ripped from the bag and tossed aside. He stops and dangles a lone pair of baby booties tied together with lace. Hurt is wrought on his face, a flexed jaw and crumpled brow that conveys a wound he does not know how to bandage. The booties remind him of what he's lost, the only good thing that could have possibly come from his union with Darlene. His eyes darken, and a breathy laugh escapes his throat. He throws the booties against the wall and starts to sob. "I wanted this to work, Darlene. I wanted to live a happy life with you, but you just had to go and ruin it! You just had to take him from me!"

"I almost died!" Darlene screams. Her pitch is so high she doesn't recognize it. Darlene looks down and holds the soft midsection of her body that grew the son they never knew. She rubs her thumb across the stretch marks on her once swollen belly, still raw and red, not yet faded to white.

"I was going to bleed out!"

"You don't know that!"

"Yes, I do! It was your hands on me, Leroy. You killed him. Not me. YOU!" She prays the vitriol from her lips stings his soul like acid rain. She prays that the truth will weaken him and force him to surrender.

Leroy stomps out of the room, and Darlene is left in silence. She looks around the closet for something to help her escape, but she doesn't have long.

Soon enough, Leroy returns, accompanied by the sound of sloshing liquid. It's a familiar sound, and so is the scent: sweet and pungent.

Gasoline.

Darlene tries to wedge the closet door open with the counterweight of her body, but it's no use. She kicks and screams, but Leroy's not listening anymore.

He's coating the room in a thick lacquer of acrimony and heartache.

PRESENT DAY

SHIRLEY TEMPLE

DARLENE LOOKS AT her handsome one-night stand, studies the hard lines of his jaw, his frame, the languid way he sits in his chair as he watches Hazel cover a Miranda Lambert song on stage. He's probably wondering what it would be like to hold Hazel's curvy hips in his hands. Jealousy burns in Darlene's heart and she knows she has no right to feel this way, but she wants him. Wants his body in a way that would snuff out any semblance of pain or thought lest she get caught in her head too long. Dampened tangled sheets. The heavy pants of animals in heat, skin clawing for skin, desperate for release—

Dark brown eyes stare back at her. He's got a shit-eating grin on his face, and it's then that Darlene realizes her mouth is wide open like a perch for birds to roost upon. She quickly turns away to fan herself with a cocktail menu.

"Hey—"

A napkin slides across the bar to Darlene. It's Brandy's friend. Her hands are shoved in her pockets, waiting for Darlene to acknowledge her.

"Hey," Darlene says, grabbing the napkin. She almost throws it out on instinct before seeing handwriting scrawled across it. It reads:

Alma Barrera
(240) 555-1935

"Oh, I'm flattered, but as a general rule I don't go out with customers."

"Is that what you tell yourself while you make sheep's eyes at them from across the room?" Alma raises her brow. Darlene's cheeks flush.

"I wasn't—"

"I don't give a shit, to be honest." Alma nods her head toward Ezra and Brandy. "What I *do* care about is my friend getting friendly with a guy who looks twice her age." She pinches the bridge of her nose. "Do you know him?"

"I know him better than most."

"And…?"

Orville looks up from his beer to lock eyes with Darlene, and she can tell he's thinking the same thing. Ezra is their friend, but still… Darlene measures her response. "Next time he goes to take a piss, ditch him. Ezra ain't a bad guy, but he ain't a great one, either, if you know what I mean."

Orville nods and goes back to his beer.

"Oh, I know exactly what you mean," Alma says. She bites her bottom lips concerned, but all Darlene sees is the lip's glossy fullness and the way it shimmers seductively under the neon light. Darlene tries not to stare, but she can't help it. Alma's eyes flick to hers, but Darlene looks away.

"This isn't the first time she's ditched me for a lay, but normally she's not leaving me in the middle of nowhere. She's a big girl, though, and I'm tired and ready to head home. Since Brandy can't get a signal out here, can you help her out if she needs it and give me a call from your landline? Just in case."

"Yeah, of course."

"Thank you," Alma says and gives Darlene's hand a squeeze. Darlene looks down at their hands linked together and meets the woman's gaze before drifting to her brown almond-shaped eyes. Darlene's cheek's flush and she retracts her hand. The woman smiles slightly.

"You sure you don't want to stay?" Darlene asks. Is she attracted to women? Yes, but it's been a while since there was anyone that caught her eye. There was that fling she met in Austin, before she met Leroy, but that was years ago. Darlene was under a dry spell when it came to women.

Perhaps it was the clientele that usually came into the garden that tempered her expectations. If it wasn't a Bible-thumping do-gooder with her husband in tow sitting on a bar stool, it was more often than not some buckle bunny who's interest in women never extended beyond a few drinks and 'accidental' kisses with their friends. *Hard pass.* Darlene wasn't willing to be someone's experiment.

She doesn't know Alma, but has surmised enough about her to know she's certainly not the former. And if she is only here for some washed-up cowboy, then she wouldn't be interested in Darlene anyway.

So why does Darlene feel disappointed about the idea of watching Alma go? And what is it about her that makes Darlene say stupid things like, *You sure you don't want to stay?*

Alma fights back a smile. "Nah, this isn't really my scene. I'm just here as a favor to Brandy. Besides, it's late and I gotta get back to the stables. Got a big race tomorrow. Can't get too crazy."

"Race? Do you do rodeo?"

"Yes ma'am." Alma squares her shoulders. "I'm a barrel racer."

Darlene smiles. "And here I was, thinking you were just another buckle bunny."

Alma giggles and bites her lip. "Oh, I don't order off *that* menu. Do you?"

Darlene feels her pulse quicken. *Get a grip. She's out of your league Darlene tells herself.*

Alma gives Darlene a wink. "I'll take that as a maybe. Thanks again…" She pauses to leave room for a name.

"Darlene."

"Darlene? Wow."

"What? It's a good name."

"Oh, it's not that. You just look more like a Dolly to me, is all."

Darlene's face feels warm. "Uh…yeah…I get that a lot."

"I bet. Listen—that number, it doesn't expire after tonight. Call me sometime. If you want."

Orville raises an intrigued eyebrow and looks to Darlene to gauge her reaction. But however she reacts, he won't press. As far as he's concerned, this ain't none of his business.

"Thanks…maybe I will." Darlene says.

Satisfied with that response, Alma impishly grins before turning on her heel to leave. Darlene does her best not to faun over the soft pleat in the woman's chestnut hair, or get lost in the outline of her ass in those jeans.

Sweat beads on Darlene's brow. *It's the rain* she tells herself. The rain always makes The Teegarden feel stuffy inside. She looks down at Alma's phone number one more time, studies it for a moment, and then pockets it. No harm in keeping it handy. Darlene knows if she's thirsty and sees a tall glass of iced tea, or a Shirley Temple, to take a sip. Life's too sweet. Maybe she needs to stop denying herself of the taste of its goodness.

IN THE RESTROOM, the window frame that's been painted over too many times to count gives way to Darlene's push, but not without resistance. A gentle breeze cools the sweat on her collarbone, providing her some relief. She peels the scarlet racerback tank top from her skin to give it room to breathe before looking at herself in the mirror. Her smokey eye shadow is smudged, and the liner is smeared and no longer sharp enough to cut a heart twice.

Great. I look like a goddamn raccoon.

After rubbing the crease of her eyelids, Darlene grabs a stack of paper towels and blots her skin. The distinct smell of wet cardboard somehow makes her feel stickier than before. She throws them away and checks her reflection in the mirror one more time.

Feathered curls fall in front of her face. She tucks the strands behind her ears, catching a glimpse of the string lights outside through the open window. Darlene's aura is red. She looks like a demon, basking in the neon-glow. She smiles, knowing how upset the holy rollers in church would be if they saw her now, and applies another layer of lip gloss. Darlene is admiring how the light accentuates her cupid's bow when movement catches her eye in the mirror. She looks up.

Someone is standing outside the window in the rain.

Darlene startles, knocking over the stack of paper towels, but when she turns around, there's no one there, just one of the many large oaks that surround The Teegarden in the grove. Darlene cracks the window more and pushes the thought of the phantom out of her mind. She's got to get a grip, catch her breath.

Darlene counts the knots of wood in the bathroom paneling: thirteen. She does this when she needs to ground herself and likes the familiarity of it. Perfectly predictable. She imagines the tree that was felled before ending up here. Unassuming, ever present, and filled with a history she will never know but somehow understands. The trees have stories to tell in the Hill Country, long after their death. They are witnesses to all that has been and continues to be, hidden from outsiders.

ON THE ROCKS

IT'S 9 P.M. Limes are low. Darlene is watching Ezra like a hawk, Hazel is belting out "Before He Cheats" by Carrie Underwood—a song and artist, Darlene hates—and the bachelorette party has turned insufferable, more painful to deal with than a rattlesnake bite.

"WOOOO! Get it girl!" one of them shouts.

The corner of Darlene's eye twitches, but she does her best not to lose it. Secretly, though, she's seeing red.

The bride, who is now standing on one of the tables, is poorly imitating the swing of a baseball bat, and the bridesmaids are singing along, cheering on their champion as she continues to smash the imaginary headlights of an imaginary car as revenge for being cheated on in her imagination. Darlene wants to point out how this is not the best sign of her coming nuptials, but she's not in the mood for a fight. Still, she has to say something. No one's allowed on the tables, for liability reasons. She steps out from behind the bar and heads over to the table where all the commotion is taking place.

"You need to get down," she says to the bachelorette, the young woman standing near ten-feet tall atop the table. *"Now."*

"Oh, come on! It's her last weekend as a free woman!" one of the bridesmaids protests. "She deserves to let loose and have a little FUN!" says another. This one is actually the Maid of Honor—identified by the cheap sash she is wearing— and she throws back another shot.

"You tell her to knock it off, or I'm kicking *all* of you out of here," Darlene warns. "This isn't one of those Nashville bachelorette parties. Those bartenders may not give a shit, but I do."

"Why are you so uptight?" says the bride from atop her perch. She smiles, but it doesn't reach her eyes. Darlene can tell that the bride's used to getting her way, and it's taking everything in Darlene's power not to yank the woman down by her hair and haul her out the door. The Maid of Honor senses this, too, and steps in.

"Come on, she's not worth getting kicked out for," she says to the bride. "We'll order another round and be on our way." The bride steps down and sneers. Darlene turns on her heels, ready to let it go, when a hand grabs her shoulder.

"What's your problem? This is *my* weekend!" the bride snarls.

Darlene knows it's the booze talking, seen this movie enough times to know. De-escalation was key. "Why don't you take a walk?" Darlene says coolly.

"In what, the rain? Maybe if you didn't have such a stick up your ass, you wouldn't be such a bent bitch. Sounds like you need a lay, or for someone to teach you a lesson!"

Bone cracks.

Darlene looks down.

Her knuckles are smeared red.

The bride tilts her head back and holds her nose, her mouth open in a shriveled "oh" as blood trickles from her nostrils like water from a leaky faucet. The bridge of her nose is already swollen and bruised.

"This nose cost six grand! Oh my God!"

"Fuck, I'm so sorry, I didn't mean to—"

"You punched her in the face?! What the fuck?" The Maid of Honor tries to console the weeping bride, who looks less like Carrie Underwood and more like Carrie White, post bucket-of-pig's-blood, but it's doing no good.

The bride fans herself with her hand. "I need air! I need air!" she shouts and the Maid of Honor spirits her outside to the porch.

The three remaining bridesmaids stir their cocktails in silence. They're more annoyed with Darlene for killing their fun than for their friend whose nose is busted a week before her wedding. Something tells Darlene that this kind of thing is a common occurrence with this group—either that, or the bride just has terrible friends. Then again, the two aren't mutually exclusive.

"Let's make this bitch pay," one of them says to the others.

"Oh, I've got an idea," says another. She climbs up onto the table and yells out to the entire bar, "Darlene here just promised everyone a round on the house! Yeah, Darlene!" When she climbs back down, she smiles wickedly at Darlene.

The crowd erupts with cheers and whistles, and Wanda glares at Darlene from the dance floor.

Great.

Darlene can't take back her punch, but at least this will set the mood right again. She's not going to worry about how much Jack Daniels is lost this round. She'll let Wanda take it out of her next paycheck. Or two.

She walks back over to the bar, leans against it, and buries her face in her hands.

"Hell of a punch you threw there, kid." Ezra says, holding Brandy by the waist.

"I don't know what came over me. She was being a brat."

"Talk shit, get hit. Some folks learn that lesson the hard way, unfortunately."

Darlene flinches. Ezra's comment stings more than he realizes. She knows what he means, but still. "Doesn't make it right."

"Yeah, but it happened. Can't worry about it now. That's tomorrow's problem."

"Am I brat, Ezra?" Brandy says in a baby voice while batting her fake eyelashes.

Ezra grins mischievously. "Darlin', you're the biggest brat in this bar."

Brandy chews her bottom lip, then starts unbuttoning Ezra's shirt with lust in her eyes. "You gonna teach me a lesson?"

Jesus Christ, she's insufferable. No wonder Alma left.

Ezra takes her hand and leads her away, the woman's laugh echoing even as they turn the corner toward the bathroom and disappear from Darlene's sight. She gags at the thought of them groping each other in the bathroom.

"I'll never understand where he gets the energy," Darlene says to Orville.

"He swears it's because he doesn't sleep in pajamas like George Strait." Orville says. His eyes narrow as he watches the reflections of Wanda and Luis dance in the gold-leaf mirror behind Darlene.

Darlene takes notice.

"Some people just know how to turn it on when it suits their needs," a stranger two seats down remarks. Apparently, he's been enjoying a side of eavesdropping while sipping his ranch water.

"Mm-hmm," says Darlene, annoyed. The look she gives the guy tells him to mind his own business or get lost—his choice. Darlene draws Orville another pour. "Hey, Orville…"

"Hmm?"

"I get why Ezra stayed single all these years. But how come you never settled down with anyone?"

"Kind of a personal question, don't you think?"

"Well, we're friends, right?"

"Of course we are."

"Then tell me."

He sighs, then rests his baseball cap on the bar. It bears the embroidered logo of his local VFW. He's been a proud member since serving in Vietnam before retiring from the Army. He doesn't talk much about his time in the service unless another veteran spots him across the bar and strikes up a conversation.

"There's a saying," he says, "that if the military wanted you to have a wife, they'd have issued you one. I dated a few gals back in the day, but none of them worked out for one reason or another. Nothing stuck. And my time in the jungles of Khe Sanh didn't help any. Kept me away a long time, and when I got back, I wasn't the same. I think the ladies noticed. It was worse for the married grunts, though. Being deployed in the '70s wasn't like how it is today; no instant text messaging down-range in your battle rattle. Watched a lot of guys end up getting divorced after twelve—*hell*—even fifteen-month deployments. Not that I blame the wives. It's hard for a marriage to survive something like that."

"And Wanda?"

Orville looks up at Darlene with a pained smile. "That one's complicated."

"How?"

"We were an item for a while. Happy, too. But I messed all that up when I enlisted."

"How so?"

"Wanda was a hippie. If she'd been born a man, she'd have been a conscientious objector. Would have burned her draft card in the streets. She couldn't understand why I'd wanna leave this place to join 'the military industrial complex' as she called it. Why I'd want to travel thousands of miles to fight in an 'unjust war.' But I was only a kid, you know? I wasn't thinking that far ahead. I just wanted to get the hell out of dodge, see the world, and never look back. " Orville's gaze returns to the reflection of Wanda. "I left; spent two tours 'in country.' Came back after the war and found out she'd left for California and met a guy."

"Henry?"

"The very same."

"And you never said anything?"

"No reason to. It just wasn't meant to be. We had our day in the sun, and she was happy with Henry. Who was I to take that away from her? I won't lie, though. I've wondered many times what life would have been like had we tried to make it work." His eyes become lost in the middle distance. "Sometimes when you meet someone, you just know there's something special about them; something in their soul that only speaks to yours. Wanda was that for me."

Darlene grabs Orville's hand and squeezes. "I get that, Orville. Really, I do."

The tender moment is cut short when a customer bellies up to the bar and orders a bucket of Coronas for him and a table of his buddies. 'Five-Dollar Friday Buckets' as Wanda had called them. After cracking the six beers open and placing them on ice, Darlene reaches beneath the bar for six limes only to discover that the tray is empty.

"I don't need 'em, sugar," the customer tells Darlene and hands her a twenty, tells her to keep the change.

"Crisis averted," says Orville.

"Very funny." Darlene looks at Orville in a new light, wanting to know more about the man behind the service ribbon embroidered on his cap. "Listen, I gotta go get some more limes from the fridge, but I'll be right back, so don't go anywhere. You and I aren't done talking yet."

HONEY TRAPPED

ANOTHER BIRD—a swallow—is now flightless, and maimed. It hobbles between structures of cedar, shiplap, and old barn equipment, where it hides from God-knows-what hunting these woods. Her throat is raw from screaming. Her mind is still in disbelief.

The torrents of rain are deafening, her cries for help unheard. She needs to get back to The Teegarden. Needs to warn them about what's coming.

The blue and pink outline of The Teegarden's famous neon sign is like a beacon in the dark. An animated cowgirl sitting atop a giant cowboy boot winks like a siren off the coast of Capri. Dangerous, yet alluring. But all the little bird can think is how they were honey trapped by 'the experience of a lifetime.'

She blames her friends for planning this trip. Blames her Maid of Honor for suggesting the middle-of-nowhere Texas because *"Western is IN"* right now. Blames all those stupid cowboy romance novels she binge-read in anticipation of their trip. She would have been just fine driving up to Scottsdale for a weekend to tan at a resort and drink mimosas with her girlfriends while trying (and failing) not to think about what her fiancé was doing with his friends in Vegas.

The bride closes her eyes and orients herself. In front of her are the saloon and outdoor dance hall. Behind her lies the unmanned gift shop. The latter is not an option, because despite its cover from the rain, it's not safe for her.

Heavy footsteps on the porch. Fox chase. Two swallows seeking shelter from danger, surrounded by tchotkes, branded apparel, and vintage Christmas ornaments in the shape of musical instruments painted with the Texas flag. Glass shatters. Blood curdling screams. Shards embedded in the eye sockets of her longest friend, dead on the floor. The searing burn of a blade on her head—

Cottonmouth. A cold sweat breaks across her skin. She doesn't know the extent of her injuries. Can't see the flap of skin still attached to the matted hair on her scalp. It all happened so fast, and she's crouching in wet dust, looking for answers, but no one is looking at her. She needs to run back to the saloon for help. The bride slows her breathing and concentrates on the path ahead.

The heavy gait of boots on gravel is all the motivation she needs.

As she runs, her satin top makes her look like a rabbit, freshly skinned, its pelt peeling away from the muscle and bone. Is the crunch beneath her white glitter-inlay boots her own, or is it the psycho who attacked her friend? The muscles in her feet whine as taut leather struggles to stretch with every stride. She should have broken them in like the sales rep told her to.

A sharp pain in her lower back, stabbing and blinding, threatens to knock her down. Pink manicured nails dig into the support beam of the outdoor dance hall. She catches her breath and looks behind her, but no one is there. She looks around only to see a pitchfork standing upright in the body of a man. Bile creeps up her throat, she doubles over, and that's when she comes face to face with a girl who has no eyes, the skin picked clean by the buzzards. June bugs flit around the corpse in pockets of light, crawling in and out of available orifices.

The bride backs away and stumbles backward onto the porch. She pushes the door open with what little strength she has left.

The silhouette of the bride clad in red, white, and mud hovers on the threshold of The Teegarden. Her scream slices through the musician's falsetto, but it doesn't matter. No one is listening to *her*. She scans the room, eyes wild, desperate to bite and thrash anything or anyone she can get her hands on because they *need* to know. Someone needs to know.

"Her eyes…" The bride's voice trails off. A gray-haired woman dancing spots her and covers her mouth in horror as she taps her dance partner on the shoulder. He turns around to see her, too, and suddenly, everyone is looking at her. What follows are the gasps of a stunned audience and the death knell of a dobro guitar.

"Her eyes…" Death looms over her like a shadow. Panic climbs up her throat and threatens to spill where she stands. Christmas lights above her look like the blurry halos of angels. Rhinestone boots scintillate and sparkle under their hue.

She grips the cross that hangs around her neck and sobs, but her prayers fall on deaf ears. There are no angels here, no emissaries for God. She's sure of that now.

Her hands are sticky against the door frame. Tacky. A sweet-smelling brown lacquer coats her fingers. The scent is pungent. Nauseating.

Blood spurts from her mouth as a horrid shrill eeks from her lips. She trembles at the sight, frozen in place. Her hands shake as she brings them to her face.

Blood. Lacquer. Sticky. Tacky. Too much. There's too much blood, mud, and whatever else is on her hands. She looks at the crowd and takes a step forward. Every movement is stiff, unnatural.

"Her eyes… SHE HAS NO EYES!"

The crowd watches in shock as she falls face-first onto the floor, revealing the handle of a hunting knife, the blade lodged deep into her back.

HUNG UP

IN THE BATHROOM, cloistered from the chaos outside, Ezra and Brandy are hot and sweaty with passion. Their fingers fight buttons and zippers, eager, starving for the sensation of skin on skin.

Doe-eyed and backed up against the wall, Brandy watches Ezra and waits. Ezra's heartbeat quickens as his body settles into the muscle memory of feverish youth. Young men are selfish, though. Too quick. Reckless with their loving, inconsiderate of a woman's needs, finishing before the going gets started. Ezra knows better than this. He knows how to pull at a woman's thread until she's about to come apart at the seams.

He leans against the wall with one hand, rubs his thumb across her lips with the other. Brandy claws for his belt, but not in the way so many buckle-bunnies had done in the past, during his heyday as a bull rider, when all they wanted was a taste of his small-town fame. Sure, maybe Brandy's mind *was* lost up there in the clouds, but there was a heart of gold beneath that red piping and fringe of hers. Ezra's never known the love of a woman, but something in the way her eyes glow under the filament bulbs makes him think that he just might be on his way.

He hoists up Brandy's pink denim skirt. She squeals, and he positions her on top of the small dresser in front of the window. He spreads her legs, playing with the hem of her underwear. Sheer. Dainty. Hardly there. As easy to peel away as it is to slice melted butter on toast.

"Ezra…" Brandy is breathless. She arches her back, grabs his hair, and writhes under his touch as he helps himself. He may never again feel the exhilaration of a crowd cheering him on beneath the bright lights of the stadium, but he can chase the sensation, the thrill, in other ways, just like he's doing now.

Every lap of his tongue brings Brandy closer to her peak. Her quick pants and muffled screams tell him she's nearly there. Faster now, his focus entirely on that spot that demands her surrender—should she give in to him. Brandy's grip on Ezra's hair loosens. She's groaning, and he takes that as a good sign. The thrill of her pleasure makes him hunger for more. Her sweetness melts in his mouth. Like the drizzle of honey on a biscuit, begging him to devour every last drop.

But then comes a different taste. Copper?

No, blood.

Ezra backs off immediately. Brandy's waist is *soaked* in blood. His eyes climb up her torso to her neck. It's severed, her eyes are rolled back, stretched wide in horror. Her mouth is frozen in a deranged twist, her lungs empty of breath.

Ezra stands. His hands tremble, unsure what to do.

"B-B-Brandy?"

The window slides all the way open.

Hands grab Ezra's neck and pull, smashing him against Brandy's face. He's hung up, caught in a straddle on top of Brandy's body because he can't see a damn thing now. He grasps the hands choking him and struggles to get his footing. He needs to pull back against the counterforce on the other side, but at this angle, he's at a disadvantage.

Brandy's body falls to the side, head-first, off the dresser, and Ezra is dragged outside the window. With his neck straddling the threshold he's unable to lift his head to see his attacker.

"I saw what you did," the attacker says, his breath hot against Ezra's ear.

"What?"

"I saw you. All of you."

"Get the fuck off me!"

"With pleasure."

The growly voice retreats, then thrusts a blade into Ezra's throat, impaling the larynx. Ezra wheezes as air seeps from the wound. Every breath is now a struggle, the sound like a whistle in the night. The blade twists, and its serrated edge saws through the left side of his neck. There's nothing humane about this killing. Ezra will not be bled out like cattle after being stunned. Ragged and quick, the cut is reckless, and that's when the pain settles in. When he feels the edge of the blade nick tendons under his jaw.

"Scream for me," the man roars.

As skin flays from his skull, Ezra lifts his chin in defiance to look his attacker in the eyes. His jaw hangs open, not to scream, but to swallow his fear whole because Ezra *knows* fear, and it sure doesn't look like this man with a mutilated face. Fear is never knowing the glory of a crowd cheering in the stands, just for him. Fear is the beady eyes of a bull, mad as hell, ready to fuck him up as soon as he opens the chute. Fear is hanging on for eight seconds to beat the clock. Even if he could scream, he wouldn't. Not now.

In his final moments, he imagines the sound of the stadium buzzer piercing the night, droning and loud. The bull is released and his eight seconds until it's all over begin. One last ride for an old cowboy.

FULL AS A TICK

SKIN ON SKIN.

Wet.

Sweet.

The gray fox sticks his tongue through Ezra's lips and licks around the mouth. He imagines he's a sand fly feasting on rotting flesh in the Texas sun. He could develop a taste for this kind of meat, he realizes. He salivates, hungry to sink his teeth into cartilage and vertebrae, but he mustn't be foolish—not when there's still so much more to do.

The fox looks in the bathroom mirror to see himself wearing Ezra's flayed face like a mask. His tongue protrudes from the cowboy's lips like a grotesque parody of Gene Simmons, or a faithful homage to Leatherface. What a great name: *Leatherface.* Should the fox give himself a new name to match?

Probably. Because he always hated his real name. Hated the man he was named after. Besides, he's not that person anymore. He's something different now. Something new. Charred. Blackened. Devoid of hope or reason. He barely remembers his former self, barely registers it as real. His name belongs to *that* man, and that man is dead.

He's down to his last knife, and the pairing blade in his hand won't be enough to take on what he's about to face on the other side of the door. He looks around the room. So many useless tchotchkes permanently adhered to the wall. Amid milk bottles and horseshoes, he spots a rusted bull holder dangling from a hook as decoration next to some rope. He hasn't needed to wrangle a calf since his granddad ran a ranch of his own out in West Texas, but he grabs both the holder and hook anyway. Muscle memory will serve him well tonight.

He looks down at Brandy's dead body on the floor and clicks his tongue. *Such a waste of a good woman.* But deep down he knows she mustn't have been *that* good. No woman really is. All of them harlots. Temptresses. He studies with disdain the too-short length of her denim skirt and how it reveals her supple thighs now smeared with blood. The whites of her eyes have rolled into the back of her head, and her neck is a gash of tattered skin and cartilage. Did she die how she lived? Subservient to sin and pleasure? If so, Eve would be proud.

The fox has lost count of the many times he's cursed God for putting him in the path of an evil woman, but no more. He has a new Father now, one who's helping the fox right the wrongs of his past. He has no more use for God.

Michelle. Randy. Ezra. He crosses their names off his mental checklist, pleased with the justice he's bestowed onto these rats. Randy should have been made to suffer longer than he did, but what is a predator to do when prey falls into its lap? It wasn't quite how the fox wanted it to go, but he's never been one to look a gift horse in the mouth.

Above the woman's body, an old hatchet hangs upon the wall by a leather strap. The whites of the fox's eyes flare, and he pants through the thin slit of Ezra's mouth. Is this a sign? Divine intervention?

He grabs the hatchet and rubs his thumb down the cutting edge. Blood beads. It's still sharp. He slashes the air with the tool, adjusting to the weight of it in his hand until it becomes another extension of himself, just like the skin he wears over his marred face. He looks at himself in the mirror once more and stares into the blueness of his eyes.

He feels whole now. New. Baptized in the blood of the wicked. He knows what to call himself now.

Hatchet. I am...Hatchet.

JAILHOUSE FREEZER

DARLENE GRABS A case of limes and hoists them to the worktable in the center of the walk-in refrigerator. Wall-to-wall, the walk-in is filled with cases of beer, wine, and condiments, many of them expired since Wanda claims expiration dates are just 'an opinion.'

Darlene grabs a box of limes and cuts them into quarters until there are more than enough wedges to refill the bar caddy she brought with her. A spray of tart citrus stings a small cut in Darlene's finger as she piles them into their tray, and she sucks the juice from the wound.

A knock comes at the door.

Strange. Wanda wouldn't knock, and no one else in the bar would have reason to come back here, so it must be a drunk needing to take a piss, Darlene reasons.

"The washroom is at the other end of the hall," she calls through the door. "But good luck with that. I think it's still occupied." Darlene tries not to let the image of Ezra and Brandy getting it on in the bathroom enter her mind. She's already going to hell for even thinking about it.

The heavy gait of a pair of boots scuffles away, followed by a soft *thud*.

Darlene hates working in the walk-in for too long. Besides leaving the bar unattended, it's the one place in The Teegarden that makes her feel small, like she's on the brink of death. She despises how the cold closes in on her the way it does, diminishes the little vitality she struggles to maintain.

Before the fire, she didn't have a problem coming in here, but now she can't stand being in this jailhouse freezer for more than five minutes at a time. Hardened hearts are quicker to freeze. She grabs the bar caddy, now heaped with sliced limes, and presses the door's release button to exit.

But it doesn't open.

Her brow furrows. She presses the button again, harder this time, but still nothing. She presses it again and again and again until, eventually, she's hammering the button with her fist. But nothing she tries works.

Shit. Shit. Shit. Shit.

Darlene's hands go numb. Her throat swells, and a cold sweat breaks across her brow. The walls start to close in on her. Great. She's trapped inside a sarcophagus of cheap beer and mayonnaise packets. The muscle under her eye twitches, and suddenly, the memories of that night all come rushing back.

The sickly-sweet smell of gasoline.

The suffocating blackness of the smoke.

The intense heat of the fire.

Darlene puts the bar caddy down and pounds her hands on the door. "Help!" she shouts. "I'm locked inside the refrigerator! Is anyone out there? Help!"

Don't panic. Don't panic. Don't. Panic.

Breathe. Breathe. Just breathe.

ONE YEAR AGO

DISRUPT

FLAMES LICK THE sky as the roof of the farmhouse collapses. The terrible sound startles Darlene, causing her to slip on the gravel as she barrels downhill toward her truck, sweaty and bleeding. Black smoke billows above. When she gets to her truck, she throws open the unlocked door and jumps inside. Keys fumble in her trembling hands before jamming the correct one into the ignition. She turns the key to start the engine, puts the S10 in reverse and pulls out onto the road.

Darlene looks up at the burning house atop the hill one last time before it's gone.

This wasn't how it was supposed to be.

She presses the gas pedal to the floor and speeds down the highway to her freedom. But the feeling of liberation is short-lived. Scenarios of a car chase between her and the police soon infiltrate her mind. She should have stayed, she laments. Should have called for help. Should have stayed until the fire department arrived. Anything to make her look less conspicuous than she does now.

It wouldn't have mattered, she tells herself.

Maybe the best thing to do would be to start over with a new name, in a new place, far away from Kimble County. The police would know she didn't perish in the fire, but she'd be long gone by then. She'd always carry the baggage of this night with her, but there's not a soul alive who doesn't have something to hide, so what does it really matter? There's always a dead body somewhere.

She stares into the yawning chasm of the night, her eyes swollen from tears, her throat raw from screaming. Every muscle in her body aches.

I'm alive. I'm alive. This is real. I'm alive.

Darlene strains to see the lines in the road. She focuses on the fence posts to guide her as fatigue threatens to shut her eyelids. Before long, the static hum of the radio lulls her into sleep. She dreams of the rolling hills of her youth, of running barefoot through the creek. Golden rays of light shine through pockets in the trees, warming her skin and glistening in the dew drops about the honeysuckles—

The blare of a car horn stirs Darlene awake, and she swerves out of the way just in time to avoid the collision. Rattled, she pulls over to the side of the road and parks. The surge of adrenaline in her blood wanes, and a hoarse cry escapes her throat. She slams the steering wheel again and again, a semiquaver of confusion, rage, and shame.

She can't just run away. She needs help. And there's only one place in town where she can find it.

Darlene pulls back onto the road and drives another five miles until the shape of The Teegarden emerges from the darkness ahead, illuminated by string lights on the porch against the mildew-stained timber siding. She parks in front of the porch and gets out but leaves the truck running. She blunders wildly into the saloon.

Darlene thanks the Lord that it's after hours on an off day since she can't bear to face strangers right now. She's welcomed into the empty bar by the soft twang of the jukebox. She shields her eyes from the glow of the neon signs, letting them readjust as she looks around.

"Wanda? Is anyone here? It's Darlene. Please, I need help. I'm in trouble."

Wanda emerges from the back with her reading glasses in hand, carrying the scent of gardenia and lilies. She lifts up her glasses to get a better look at the hour on the clock before returning to Darlene's stare. Wanda rests her forearm on the counter before pouring them both a double shot of Jim Bean.

"What kind of trouble?"

PRESENT DAY

ARMED TO THE TEETH

DARLENE FEELS AROUND the refrigerator door frame for a way out. If she's lucky, she can finagle something between the door and the frame to use like a hinge. She stares at the knife in her hand.

"Sorry, Wanda."

Darlene wedges the knife into the door frame and pulls. There's tension but not enough leverage. She tries again.

"Hello? Is anyone there?" The cold sweat returns, and Darlene's vision blurs. Her hand cramps up, and the cut on her finger splits further.

Then, just like before, boots scuff the linoleum and pause outside the door.

Darlene yells louder and bangs with both hands against the galvanized steel. "Hey! Can you hear me? I'm trapped in here! Please, let me out!"

"Darlene? Is that you? Oh, thank God you're all right. We've been lookin' everywhere for you." The sound of Orville's drawl is music to her ears.

"Orville! Yes, I'm all right. Just a little stuck at the moment." Darlene lets out a good hearty laugh of relief.

"Hang tight," Orville says. "Something's in the way."

The sound of something heavy scrapes against the door as it's pulled out of the way. Had someone intentionally blocked her exit?

The bridesmaids…

They did say they would make Darlene pay. They were probably the ones who knocked on the door, too, in an effort to scare Darlene. How petty could those spoiled brats be?

Moments later, Orville opens the door. He's got Levi, who's playing dead, tucked under his arm. Orville catches his breath and hands Levi over to Darlene. The opossum immediately reanimates, and his little paws clutch the hem of her tank top. Darlene tucks the knife in her apron pocket and embraces her friend.

"That right there is why you were trapped," Orville says, pointing to a pushcart stacked high and wide with bulk boxes of Tennessee whiskey.

"Unbelievable!" Darlene grumbles.

"Darlene—" Orville says.

"They have no idea who they're messing with. They don't make women like me in Scottsdale—"

"Darlene—"

"You think Randy still keeps that shotgun of his in his truck?"

"Darlene!" Orville places his hands on her shoulders. "Randy's dead!"

Darlene's face goes blank. "What do you mean he's dead?"

For the first time since exiting the fridge, she notices that the band has stopped playing. And instead of laughter coming from the dance hall, she hears shouting.

"Michelle's dead, too," Orville says. The words feel like a lie on his lips, but he knows they're not. His brain just can't fully believe them yet.

"That doesn't make any sense. Michelle's not even here, she's supposed to be in Austin." Darlene glares at him with daggers in her eyes. "This isn't funny, Orville. Did those heifers put you up to this? Is this just another part of their little prank? I gotta say, I thought better of you."

"I ain't jokin', Darlene." The tears welling up in his eyes make Darlene's blood run cold. She's never seen Orville cry, not even in jest. As crazy as it sounds, the man is telling the truth.

Darlene pushes past Orville and sprints toward the dance hall. When she rounds the corner, her footsteps come to a halt—a maelstrom of chaos has overcome The Teegarden. People are rushing around, pushing, shoving, and literally stepping over one another to get to the exits. Across the room, the body of a dead woman lies facedown on the floor, a knife protruding from her back. At first, Darlene thinks it's Michelle, but then she recognizes the hair, the outfit, the boots.

It's the bride.

A hand grabs hold of Darlene's elbow, and she jumps. But when she whirls around, she sees Orville.

"Darlene! Don't!" he pleads. "It's not safe. Wanda told me to head to the office and call the police, so that's what you and I are gonna do. Together."

"Oh my God…" A sob catches in Darlene's throat. "Who… Who did this?"

"Darlene. The phone."

Darlene tears her arm away from Orville. "Who did this?!" she demands. Her mind is spinning from all the horrible possibilities, and it won't begin to settle until it first knows the truth. Levi tucks his snout into the crook of her neck and trembles.

Orville shakes his head, unsure of what to say. "Darlene, I… I don't know. But whoever it is, they're still on the loose."

Darlene wants to scream, wants to pull fistfuls of hair from her head, but instead her legs betray all instincts and leads the two of them back down the hallway toward the office. Before she gets there, though, she sees blood on the floor just outside the bathroom door.

Ezra, she panics. And without thinking, she opens the door and steps inside. But after taking one look at the massacre, she turns and immediately stumbles back out again, gagging profusely at the sickening sight and smell.

"Keep moving," Orville says in a hushed whisper. He doesn't check the bathroom. Doesn't need to. Darlene's reaction tells him enough. Still, he draws his Glock from its holster and holds the weapon at the ready.

When they reach the office, they find the door unlocked but the room empty. Orville grabs the telephone receiver from off Wanda's desk and puts it to his ear. But before he starts dialing 9-1-1, he stops. "We have a problem," he says.

"Don't tell me—"

"The phone line is dead." He lifts the phone cradle to show Darlene that the cord to the wall has been severed. The Teegarden is cut off from the outside world.

PSYCHO

HYSTERIA SWEEPS ACROSS the dance hall as drunk patrons stampede for the exits like a heard of longhorns. For all the bull riders in the bar, the hardest eight seconds of their lives begins now.

"I told you this bar was a shithole," Tim says to Hazel, still clutching his dobro guitar as the pair stand like deer in the headlights onstage.

"This 'shithole' is a country music mecca," Hazel retorts.

"Oh yeah? Then why the fuck don't they have cell service? It's like we're stuck in 1975."

"Don't give me that," Hazel says. "You were all about this gig when we booked it."

Their gaze drifts to the bachelorette party nearby, still screaming over the loss of their friend. Hazel just wants to leave, but Tim wants to get paid before they go.

"A couple hundred bucks is not worth getting murdered over, let's just *go*."

"We're in the middle of fucking nowhere, our van is on empty, and we have no money for gas. How exactly do you propose we leave without first getting paid?"

"I don't know. Let's just go as far as the van will take us."

"And get stranded on the side of the road with a killer on the loose? What a great idea!" Tim mocks. The sarcasm in his voice is thick. "I'm not going anywhere until that bartender comes back out." He sips on his rum and coke and stares blankly across the bar at a St. Pauli's girl, the illustrated poster girl beaming in a blue checkered dirndl with two steins in one hand. Hazel wants to smack the plastic cup out of Tim's mouth, but she can't take her eyes off the bride's dead body.

Besides the few patrons with seemingly direct connections to the deceased, nearly everyone has cleared out of the The Teegarden by now, or is in the desperate act of doing so. And here she stood, just waiting, all because her and Tim were too broke to buy gasoline ahead of time. She glares at the guitar player and suddenly thinks she hates the man she's shackled herself to in holy matrimony.

Hazel had been looking forward to this trip for months now, but her husband's negative attitude ever since leaving the comforts of their home near Charleston has made the experience unbearable. This trip was supposed to be good for them, something to ignite the spark that had been snuffed out by the stress and uncertainty of three dead-end jobs, all on different shifts. The couple hardly saw each other back home, and when they did, it was in passing. To make matters worse, the housework (cooking, cleaning, repairs) all seemed to all fall on her shoulders and not his. The last thing she wants to be is Tim's mother, but someone needs to take out the trash, and she knows it won't be him.

She's so tired. They were just teenagers when they met, looking to blaze their way into a world they were told wasn't made for them, and she's been at a loss for what to do without him ever since. Too poor to leave, but too unhappy to stay. The thought of traveling through the south to sing at dive bars and honky-tonks stirred something in both of them, though. Something they both longed for, separately but also together. Maybe their shared love of music, head-banging, and rocking out for a crowd of people under bright lights was exactly what the marriage counselor ordered. This string of shows was going to make them feel sixteen again.

Hazel thinks of her mother, the woman that could somehow do it all with a smile on her face. *The drugs, it was the drugs*, she reminds herself. Uppers gave her mother the stamina of a wild horse, which she needed in order to clean the house, cook three-square meals a day for her family, and attend every parent-teacher function at school without cracking. That was until the drugs started to lose their effectiveness and her mother quickly declined—

She pushes down the thought. No sense in thinking about the past now, not when she should be here in the moment thinking of an exit strategy. Hazel could say 'fuck it all' and leave Tim to fend for himself. There's a quarter tank in the van; she can get far enough to find a gas station, use whatever's left in her bank account (the one she keeps hidden from Tim) and keep driving west toward a new life.

She forces herself to look away from the bride's corpse and up at the paper stars dangling from the rafters. There's something about the way the stars capture the glow of the Christmas lights and electric signs that makes her feel like she's in a neon dream tonight. Maybe it's the framed autographs or tacky memorabilia, but she feels on the precipice of something life-changing. A new beginning.

Hazel will be brave tonight. If she makes it out of here alive, she will leave Tim for good. Let whoever's left sort out the mess left behind. It's none of her business anyway.

A fist pounds on the jukebox near the bar, and Hazel snaps out of her daydream to look over at the man responsible. His lanky limbs are disproportionate to his figure, and his face is a malformed sheet of skin stretched too tight across his angular features. Why does she know that face? Was he the old guy dancing with the much younger woman? Yeah, she thinks he is.

He stares back at her, but his gaze is hollow. Without soul. And that's when Hazel sees it.

The hatchet in his hand.

She opens her mouth to scream but no sound comes out. A bluebird without song. Her outstretched fingers flutter against Tim's skin, desperate for his attention, but he's too obsessed with refreshing the internet app on his phone to care.

Over at the bar, Hazel sees Wanda clinging to Luis for safety as he checks the cylinder of his Magnum revolver for bullets. The man from the jukebox is heading their way. Sensing as much, the two look up to watch him approach.

"Jesus Christ…" Luis mumbles. "Is that…?"

"Oh my God…" says Wanda. "Ezra!" She falls off her bar stool at the sight of her friend's face being worn as a mask and struggles to get to her feet.

Luis locks the chamber of his revolver and points. "Stay back!" he shouts.

"Luis, wait—"

But Luis doesn't hesitate. He pulls the trigger and the pistol's strong recoil sends him back a step. The shot is deafening, and Hazel thinks her eardrums have burst. She slams her hands to her ears and drops down into a crouch.

Wanda screams.

When Hazel looks up again, Luis is dead where he lays, his neck hacked and pouring out like a gully washer.

The killer turns to Wanda, who has regained her footing. A bullet wound in his shoulder gushes blood, but he doesn't seem to mind. "Wanda Higgins..." he sneers. A wry laugh escapes his throat like hag moths fluttering out of a rotting cadaver.

Wanda grabs a leftover bottle of Shiner Bock and smashes it against the counter to make the bottom end jagged. She stands, homemade weapon in hand, ready for what comes next.

"Back up!" Tim shouts, stepping between Wanda and Luis's killer.

Hazel hasn't seen this side of him in years. Either he wants to get paid real bad, or he's had an epiphany and decided to actually caring about others more than he does himself.

Hatchet smiles, his teeth sharp as daggers, gums as red as fresh game skinned for the fire.

Time stills.

It's the smell of metal that hits her first. The tang on Hazel's tongue tastes like pennies, and she realizes there's blood splatter on her glasses. She haphazardly wipes it off with the cuff of her sleeve and is left with the sight of their husband clutching at his throat as blood spurts in every direction.

Tim's looking at her, wide-eyed, begging her to run. She *should* run. Why can't she run? Why is she frozen in place, watching her husband die a grisly death inside some lonely Texas bar, a thousand miles from home?

Tim topples over onto the floor. Blood pools underneath his head, staining the linoleum. Hazel is caught in a fever dream of dazzling lights and violence. She should scream, should run, but instead she fixates on the twinkle of the Christmas lights reflected in her husband's blood. She opens her mouth to say something, but her voice cut short by the burn of a hatchet hacked into her belly.

Hatchet is on top of her now, grinning maniacally behind his skin-mask. Blood curdles up into Hazel's mouth as her body rejects the violence. She spits blood and warily raises an arm up to strike her attacker, but all he does is grab it. She's pushing her weight against him now, trying to force him off her body, but he's too strong, and her own strength is quickly waning.

The grip of his hand is painful against her wrist until a crackling sound lets her know he's splintered the bone there in two. Hazel looks into his eyes. She wants him to know her rage. Wants him to know she died fighting. She swipes at his cheek with her nails and claws the ungodly skin-mask off on one side. It hangs from the man's real face like queso dripping off chips.

The man's eyes are blue. The same color as her mother's face when she found her dead on the living room floor with an empty bottle of pills beside her. He wraps a hand around her throat and squeezes her larynx with all his might until it's crushed beneath the force. Hazel begins to choke. As the blood sputters onto her chest, the man releases her wrist and yanks the hatchet out of her stomach.

Hazel focuses on the dangling lights above her until she no longer feels the pain of the axe chopping up her intestines like pulled pork. She turns her head toward Tim bleeding out on the floor next to her.

Tim's eyes lock on Hazel's. He reaches for her, and there's clarity in his dying breath that tells Hazel this is the first time he's seen her, truly seen her, in years, and he *does* love her. He's always loved her.

The last thing Hazel sees is the hatchet split the side of Tim's skull.

RHINESTONE COWBOY

HATCHET'S BLADE SINGS. Blood sprays. Bodies cascade, splay like splattered bugs on a windshield in every direction as he dances across the room in a death spiral. Denim and fringe fold into one another like a patchwork quilt of fabric and skin. All that remains is the beaten pulp of flesh and bone.

Sequin sparkles in meat. Curious. Dazzling. An invitation to try, Hatchet picks up the bedazzled Stetson hat and places it upon his crown. He's a *real* rhinestone cowboy now, and he has finally arrived.

Hatchet sucks the crimson delight off his fingers, like BBQ sauce on brisket. For so long he's been a scavenger, a vulture feasting on highway carrion as he prepared for this special night.

The exit wound from the bullet that punched through Hatchet's shoulder blade sears like flank steak on cast-iron. The loss of blood has started to make his arm go numb. Maybe this is part of God's punishment for him. Hatchet knows he's a sinner, he just no longer cares. He admits to laying with women who were not his wife and succumbing to the base desires of the flesh. He knows it was wrong, but he rationalizes it anyway—claims his heart stayed loyal, just not his loins. He knows God made him, but also that He did so with malice. Why else would an all-powerful thing curse his children with the infinite capacity for sin? It wasn't the snake that lied to Eve in The Garden. It was Him.

Hatchet will make this right, though. He'll suck the poison from this place, and banish all the evils that led his life astray. Every sin, after all, stems from rotten roots.

He grabs a tea light candle from one of the high tops and holds the flame next to a wall that's he'd already lacquered with gasoline the night before. One would think an establishment like the The Teegarden would have better security…

Ignorance is a sin, too.

With a whisper of cinder and the curl of a flame, fire engulfs the dance hall. The spinning disco ball in the rafters mirrors the dismantling force of nature until the heat warps and melts its plastic shell. Every paper star goes supernova in a flash of fiery light. Here in this place, Hatchet is God, and the prophecy of Revelations is at hand.

His gummy smile of scarred muscle and tendons stretches wide. He hopes Darlene likes the gesture, but will it be enough? He doesn't have time to buy flowers, but he can still write her a card.

KEROSENE BLUES

DARLENE STROKES LEVI'S wiry hair, paying extra attention to the flap of skin behind his ears. She adjusts the cute little cowboy hat that's held on with a hair barrette, and feigns a reassuring smile at him.

But the moment ends when the boom from a Magnum revolver goes off from somewhere out in the bar.

"We can't stay here," Orville says.

"And go where? Out there? How do we know it's just one guy? There could be more than one killer out there."

"Maybe, but if we don't move, we're sitting ducks."

"I don't have a gun."

"No, but you have a knife."

"A dull one." Darlene doesn't want to fight with something less deadly than a butter knife.

"There's gotta be something in here we can use," he says, picking his teeth with a toothpick.

Acrid smoke seeps into the office from beneath the closed door, and the two crinkle their noses at the smell. Orville taps the metal door handle to feel for heat and discovers that it's already quite hot.

"There's a fire out there."

A cold sweat washes over Darlene. The nerves under her eyes and in her lips twitches. She can't feel her face. She strokes Levi's hair, but her hands don't feel like hers. This body, *her* body, feels more like a prison she needs to escape from.

Thin slats. The undertow of rum and gasoline. Smoke. Heat. "Darlene? Darlene!"

"I'm here," she says without looking at Orville. Darlene continues to focus on Levi's salt and pepper coat as her compulsive strokes start to bring out his musk. Levi doesn't flinch under her touch and presses into her body for comfort.

"I need you to pay attention. Stay with me, Darlene. We're going to get out of this, okay?" Orville sets his gun down on the desk and places a hand on top of Darlene's. Warmth radiates from his skin, the steadiness of which calms Darlene's nerves. She meets his gaze.

"Can you do that for me? Can you be here with me now as my battle buddy?" Past worry lines and gold-rim glasses, a younger version of Orville shines through, calm and resolute in the face of grave danger.

Darlene nods and releases a breath, long and drawn out. She lifts her hand from Levi's back. Even though her skin is still clammy, and her nerves still twitch in her face, the tingling sensation in her skin has resolved.

"Good. You're doing real good. You're Darlene-*fucking*-Boone. You're a fighter, just like me. Now let's get the hell out of here."

Hands rap on the office door. Darlene and Orville steel themselves, gripping their weapons tight.

"Hello? Please, is anyone in there?" Wanda rasps from the other side. "It's so hard to breathe."

Without hesitation, Orville opens the door and pulls Wanda into the room before slamming the door closed again.

The two lock eyes for a moment until Wanda looks down at Orville's gun and takes a step back. He sees the Magnum revolver she holds in her own hand and raises his eyebrow.

"I was worried you both were dead," she says.

"I was worried, too," says Darlene, and she leans into Wanda in a one-armed hug.

"Ezra? Have you seen Ezra?" Orville asks, his voice brusque.

Wanda grimaces as tears well in her eyes. She throws her arms around Orville's neck and wraps him up in her arms. She lays her head on his shoulder and begins to sob.

Orville runs a calloused hand through Wanda's hair and holds her tight, as if she'll fall completely to pieces the moment he lets go.

"Time to go!" Darlene reminds them. "This place is getting ready to collapse!"

Orville nods and grabs Wanda by the hand, then leads both women into the fray.

SMOKE BILLOWS INSIDE The Teegarden, leaving a thick black residue on all the priceless memorabilia. Flames lick the wood beams above. One by one, Christmas lights burst, and colored glass rains from the ceiling like fireworks in the night sky. In the middle of the floor is a hand-carved message, the letters of which have been set ablaze:

HAPPY ANNIVERSARY

Amid the death and destruction, a man is finishing a giant exclamation point with the edge of his hatchet while singing his own rendition of Gary Stewart's "She's Acting Single."

Darlene's heart drops. Husky, velvet, and growly, she'd know the sound of that voice anywhere.

"Leroy," Darlene's voice hitches. "It's him."

Leroy drops his hatchet and walks toward her, his cheeks bleeding as he tries to smile. He opens his arms wide and holds them there, in hopeful anticipation of her embrace. Flames hug the outline of his figure, making him look like a devil who's just come up from Hell.

"Miss me, Sunflower?"

Darlene backs up. Her chest heaves and she grinds her teeth as dizziness threatens to overcome her.

"Look at me." His voice is hoarse, barely a whisper. "Look at me, *Darlene.*"

The venom that drips from his tongue tastes so familiar to Darlene that it scares her. She looks into her dead husband's eyes: ice-blue with golden flecks. She's reminded of joyrides through the countryside and a night of passion that led her to the pits of hell and back. Darlene's knees lock up.

"I…don't understand," she stammers. "You're supposed to be dead."

"According to who? Wanda?"

Darlene turns to look at her mentor and friend. The pain in the old woman's eyes is enough to break her. "What's he talking about?" Darlene doesn't want to believe it, but knows there's truth to what Leroy is saying.

Wanda clams up, grabs Orville's bicep for support.

"Yeah, Wanda," Leroy jeers. "What *am* I talking about?"

"Wanda?" Darlene whispers.

"Come now, Wanda," Leroy says. "Tell her what you did. What *all* of you did."

ONE YEAR AGO

WHEN IT RAINS

FAILURE.

The word echoes in Leroy's mind. What did he miss? How could he not know Darlene wanted to leave him for good? Tears stream down his cheeks.

Failure.

He should have been a better husband. He should have kept his hands off other women. Should have spared his wife of all his anger. What kind of man strikes a woman the way he does?

Failure.

Visions of Darlene cloud his mind. Visions of her barreling through dust and oak while branches tugs at her T-shirt in an effort to turn her back; to save him. Darlene is *good*. Darlene is *kind*. She'll do the right thing…

She won't, though. And why should she? After all the hell he put her through? If he were a stronger man, he'd do the right thing: pull the gun out of his nightstand, stick it in his mouth, and pull the trigger.

If.

But he isn't.

Leroy holds a broken bottle in his hand. Doesn't notice the amber shards sticking out of his arm. His body is numb and his head is fuzzy; he's still drunk.

Failure.

Sobering truths can be found at the bottom of a bottle. Darlene is gone. First thing she'll do is head to the police, he's sure of it. Tell them what he did. Could Leroy say it was just a joke? That he wasn't seriously going to burn the house down? That he just wanted to scare her? The same kind of excuses have worked before.

Failure comes at the cost of infernal sorrow.

Leroy always wanted to love a woman the way they do in those old Westerns, but how could he love Darlene that way when she never needed saving? The idea that she would never truly need him terrified him, and over time, he let that fear take control. His physicality became his refuge. She might be able to run, but she'd never be able to fight, and it was only because of his divine mercy that she'd never have to feel the full power of his wrath. She was lucky like that.

Maybe he should just stay down. Sit in this hallway, let himself pass out from the smoke and burn alive. Die from suffocation. He wouldn't feel a thing by that point. His life didn't matter anymore, not now after he'd gone too far? Nothing good waited for him on the other side of that threshold. Let his body incinerate and turn to ash. Let his remains be scattered by the winds. Let him be free of his worldly torment for good.

A voice calls out through the smoke.

"Leroy! Leroy, where are you?"

He knows this voice. Knows it to be Randy Hoffman, the farmer from the orchard nearby. In a previous life, they'd share drinks at The Teegarden, he and his buddies Orville and Ezra. That was until he got with Darlene, the rookie bartender under Wanda's wing. Until her bruises became too recognizable, and they finally stepped in. Leroy should have learned his lesson, but he didn't. It only made him angrier.

"I'm here!" Leroy coughs. *"I'm here!"* He's so weak. So tired of being mean. He prays for Randy to end him here and now, put him down like a rabid dog.

Randy emerges from the smoke and reaches for Leroy, slings the man's arm over his shoulder, and together they hobble out of the house. When they finally get outside, Leroy gasps. He's never loved the sensation of clean air in his lungs more than he does now.

Randy guides Leroy to his K5 Blazer. Michelle, his daughter, sits in the driver's seat clutching the steering wheel so tight her knuckles are white. She doesn't look at Leroy. Leroy tries not to look at her because he knows she knows what he did.

Orville and Ezra stand on opposite sides of the SUV, arms crossed, waiting for him to get in the cab. Maybe Darlene called them to help.

Maybe she doesn't hate him after all.

He could only be so lucky.

Leroy sits between Orville and Ezra in the back while Randy sits up front and Michelle drives. She keeps her eyes forward as the K5 kicks up dust and night sweeps over the open road. Gravel crunches under the tires as she veers off the service road onto a private dirt path, barely wide enough for the K5 to drive between the trees. Leroy doesn't know the way they're going. Someone's ranch, perhaps?

"I'm so thirsty," he says.

"I'm sure you are," says Randy.

Leroy feels safe now, knows he'll get through this. If he could just talk to Darlene and apologize, say he's sorry, that he'll never do it again… All these thoughts in his head tire him out, and soon, he shuts his eyes—

"WAKE UP, YOU sumbitch!"

Leroy wakes to find himself upright and tied to a tree. He immediately smells smoke.

"Thought you'd get off easy?" Randy says, stepping forward into Leroy's periphery. He's holding a gas can as red as a fire hydrant, and he pours that pungent-sweet liquid Leroy knows so well at his feet.

Orville and Ezra appear and they lay into Leroy with all they've got—punch after punch until the man's body is made tender like veal. Leroy's sure the bones in his face are shattered. He looks up to see the stars through the swollen slits of his eyes. Michelle sits on the hood of the K5 and smokes a cigarette. She could care less about Leroy's suffering, because in her mind, he deserves it.

Is this justice, though? He was willing to pay for his crimes and die on his own terms inside that burning house, but somehow that wasn't enough.

Enough for who, though?

Why do these four get to decide?

They don't stick around to watch, though. After igniting the fire, they hop back into the K5 and speed off down the road. Leroy is alone and unimportant in the most monumental of ways. Even the wild javelina steers clear of the embers that stir beneath his feet. Does Darlene know where he is? Leroy hates that he's naive enough to think she cares.

The flames of his funeral pyre climb slowly up his legs and soon engulf the tree. The wind picks up, fanning the smoke. His airway feels like a pinched straw. Flames sting his skin.

Leroy tries to muster the Lord's Prayer, but words fail him. His intention is lost in the confines of his mind as he swishes saliva to relieve his cottonmouth. He licks his lips. Keeps the moisture from evaporating until the nerves of the outermost layer of skin burn away.

Blisters bubble and swell on pink as heat continues to melt flesh. Everywhere hurts, but Leroy cannot scream. Not in the way he needs to. Whatever noise he makes is more animal than human, primordial and all consuming. He can no longer discern the pain of the surface burns from the pain deep in his bones as skin sloughs away from muscle. His body expels what it can from both ends as it struggles to survive the shock. As it fails to survive the burns.

There's that word again: *Failure.*

"Sorry" will never be enough.

As the pain overwhelms him and threatens to pull him under, lightning strikes and thunder roils. The sky opens up, drizzles, then drowns the arid earth in a downpour. The torrent beats down in sheets and smothers the fire until it dies out. Leroy thinks he's drowning until finally, he comes up for air.

Born again, a child of violence, fervor, and revenge.

PRESENT DAY

PASS ME BY

"THE RAIN... SAVED me," Leroy tells Darlene "A storm so furious, I was sure it was God redeeming my soul for what I'd done, but I was wrong. It wasn't God who saved me. It was the Devil, and he was finally calling me home. Remaking me, shaping me into something new; something in *his* image." Leroy takes a step closer, careful with his dropped foot as it slaps the floor. "Don't you see now, Darlene? God abandoned me. He left me long ago. But I have been shown a new path toward freedom, one that is paved with truth and *justice*." He seethes.

Darlene looks to Wanda with tears in her eyes.

"I—I'm sorry," Wanda stammers. "You were never supposed to know."

"I scabbed and starved in those woods, Darlene," Leroy says. "But I did it all for you. I needed to see you again, tell you I'm sorry for what I'd done. I'm a changed man now, see? I can finally be the husband you deserve."

A piece of flaming wreckage falls from the ceiling and crashes to the floor, which causes Leroy to be distracted just long enough for Orville to raise his Glock and fire. But the recoil never comes. The gun just clicks. The magazine is empty, Orville remembers. He forgot to reload it after the last time he went to the range.

Enraged by Orville's gumption, Leroy grabs the old man by his neck and clips the bull holder to his septum. He yanks hard on the bull holder and slams Orville face-first to the ground, breaking his nose and sending his eyeglasses skidding across the floor. He then drags the stunned man to the famous bow and fiddle that once belonged to Charlie Daniels that now hangs proudly on The Teegarden's wall. Leroy pulls the bow from the wall and thrusts the pointed end directly into Orville's eye, deep enough to skewer it like a shish kebab.

"Orville!" Wanda screams.

Leroy rips the bow from Orville's eye socket taking the eyeball with it, then tosses it aside into the flames. Orville doubles over, hands clutching his bloody face.

"You were right about one thing, Darlene," Leroy says as he raises his small axe into the air. "Leroy's dead." He brings the blade down onto the back of Orville's neck, causing the man to immediately go limp in a spray of blood and spinal fluid. Leroy chops away at the body again and again until Darlene's and Wanda's bloodcurdling screams are reduced to helpless whimpers.

"There's only this!" he screams, raising the bloodied axe high. "Only me! Only *Hatchet!*"

BOOM!

It's the sound of a Magnum.

Leroy drops to the floor, after taking a .357 slug right to the chest. Darlene watches his body, waits for the rise of his back to show he's still breathing, but the swell of air never comes.

She looks over to see Wanda holding the smoking gun. *Not much of a pacifist, after all.* Mascara runs down her cheeks like ash on birch. She shoots four more slugs into

Leroy's fallen corpse and then clicks the trigger three more times for good measure, even though the cylinder had already been emptied.

Wanda drops the gun and rushes over to Orville. She falls to her knees and cradles his butchered skull against her breast. Her body heaves as she rocks him back and forth. She whispers sweet nothings and sorrowful regrets. "I'm so sorry," she says between sobs. "For everything."

"Why'd you do it, Wanda?" Darlene asks.

"Do what?"

"Have them kill Leroy!"

Wanda's lips tremble. "He deserved to suffer for what he did to you!"

"At what cost?" Darlene cries. "Look around, Wanda! They're all dead now! All because of *you*!" Darlene looks away, disgusted. "All because of me…"

"Don't you say that!" Wanda snaps. She sets Orville down and stands, then grabs Darlene's shoulders. "What I did was wrong, Darlene. I know that now, and if we make it out of here alive I'll spend the rest of my life atoning for that. But we're *family*, Darlene. *You* and *me*. And we protect our own! Don't you ever let that sumbitch take that light, that love, away from you."

Darlene collapses into Wanda's arms and cries.

"I love you, Darlene. And I will always fight for you."

Levi releases a high-pitched mewl.

He's right, Darlene reckons. They need to get out of here quick, before the roof comes down on them. She searches the dance hall for an easy exit, for any way out that isn't already on fire or blocked by absolute carnage. The bride-who-almost-was and her gaggle of butchered friends lay stacked on top of one another in front of the main door, and Darlene's one-night stand, still nameless, is folded over a shattered window, his torso impaled on a two-foot shard of broken glass. Intestines hang, coiled, from his open belly, like rope that's been hung from a saddle.

They can push his body over the sill and exit out the window after him.

"This way!" Darlene says.

Wanda takes her hand, and together they rush to the window. Before shoving her ex-lover's dead body over the sill, Darlene tosses Levi over the cadaver and out the window to safety. The drop is a mere three feet, and Levi lands on his paws without issue, but for some reason, his instinct doesn't kick in. He doesn't run away. Levi just stands still, looking back at Darlene, confused, as if waiting for her to join him.

"Go!" Darlene shouts. "Get out of here, Levi!"

The opossum backs away far enough to be safe from the growing flames, but not far enough to lose total sight of Darlene.

"Okay, you're next." Darlene says to Wanda. "But first I gotta clear the way."

She grabs the skewered man by his boots and lifts, then pushes toward the window until the shard of glass that impales him breaks free from the window frame. He topples—glass still inside him—out the window in a heap.

Levi hisses at the dead body after it hits the ground.

"Just be careful of the broken glass," Darlene tells Wanda as she helps her over the sill.

But before Wanda can completely clear the obstacle, a lasso catches her ankle, tightens, and then yanks her back inside. She hits the floor hard enough to knock the wind completely out of her.

Darlene looks back to see Leroy, risen from the dead and on his feet, holding the other end of the lasso and pulling Wanda toward him. He bends down and fists her hair, lifts her head until she's on her knees, then holds her face close to the fire.

"How does that feel?" he barks. "The heat melting your skin? Now you know what I felt like, tied to that fucking tree!"

Leroy lifts Wanda by her armpits and slams her back against the wall with such force she coughs blood. When she looks down, she sees one of Rusty's horns protruding from her chest. Leroy releases his grip on her and lets her hang like a crooked picture from the taxidermized bust.

Darlene shrieks at the sight. The world falls away around her in a kaleidoscope of fire and glass, obscuring her periphery. Right now, it's just her and Wanda suspended in this moment of time.

Between coughs of blood and the final throws of death, Wanda manage to lock eyes with Darlene. Her death rattle is a string of words forced from trembling lips.

"BURN…HIM. BURN…THAT…FUCKER…TO…THE…GROUND!"

She wails as the flames from the wall overtake her.

Leroy smiles at the spectacular sight.

ONE YEAR AGO

HONKY TONK ANGELS

DARLENE SITS IN the small kitchenette of Wanda's home, surrounded by cast iron skillets hanging on the wall and paintings of a ranch whose name is forgotten now. It's all too familiar to her. There's a smell of cinnamon, butter, and toast wafting in her nostrils, and she can't help but choke back the sobs bubbling in her throat. She and Wanda have sat in silence for almost ten minutes now.

She watches Wanda flip the toast in the pan, grateful to be a guest at her table. She didn't have to drive Darlene to her home, but she did. Wanda slides the toast in front of her and crinkles her nose. Acrid and smoky, Darlene can smell the soot in her hair.

Darlene curls over and gently lays her head on the table. The plastic film from the tablecloth sticks to her face. She's a wounded bird, tired of flying, fighting the pain that's in her wings.

"Eat up, now. It's all right, you're safe here."

"I killed him," Darlene whispers, like a quiet confession just loud enough for the Lord to hear. Wanda says nothing and rubs Darlene's back, waits for her to take a bite of the toast she had made. Darlene absently gazes at the gingham tablecloth, and replays the night in her head once more. It all happened so fast.

"Lift your head up outta that puddle you've made and tell me, are you okay? Show me where you're hurt."

"But I just said I–"

"I know what you said, but you look beat up real bad, so first I'm going to ask again, are you okay?"

Darlene hesitates for a moment. "Yes."

"Do you want me to take you to the hospital?"

"No! Please don't." Darlene shakes. "I can't go back there. *Won't* go back there. The last time I went to the hospital I almost died…the doctors were too scared to intervene." She inhales sharply. "I hemorrhaged, went into shock…and his heart stopped beating. I survived. He died."

Wanda doesn't have to ask who "he" is. She knows Darlene's talking about her unborn son.

"I didn't get to name him." Darlene whispers.

"Leroy deserved this, Darlene. It was self-defense."

"I don't… I just… " Darlene doesn't know how to say the words. Her lips quiver and she casts her eyes away. "He was gonna kill me. He locked me in a closet and set the house on fire."

Darlene closes her eyes and recounts the worst night of her life to Wanda. How Leroy dragged her into the bedroom and locked her inside the closet. How, in spite of the furniture leaning against the door, Darlene was able to push the door open just enough to fit through the small opening. How she saw Leroy standing in the bedroom doorway, crying, with a half-drunk bottle of beer in his hand.

Darlene's bottom lip trembles. "I just left him there. I don't know why, but I did. He's probably dead by now. Burned alive because of me."

"Now you listen here. You stop feeling sorry for that sumbitch right now. Don't you ever apologize for defending yourself and doing what you need to survive."

Darlene rests her head in her hands. "I don't know what to do, Wanda. You think I can go to prison for this?"

"Don't you worry about that right now. You're tired. Take the bed in the guestroom and get some rest. I'm gonna stay up, make a few calls. I'm gonna take care of this."

Wanda sits, holds Darlene's hands, and squeezes.

"You know why I call you Wildflower, Darlene? Wildflowers are resilient. They can grow just about anywhere, blooming in places they shouldn't; places you would never expect. You understand what I'm saying don't you? You're not just some victim; you're a survivor. You're a fighter, goddamnit."

PRESENT DAY

WHITE PICKET FENCE

DARLENE WATCHES WANDA burn. "What am I gonna do without you?" she whispers. She feels warm breath on her ear.

"Just the two of us now," Leroy grunts.

Darlene grabs the knife from her apron, but Leroy grabs her wrist and twists until her grip on the weapon fails. He pins her other hand behind her back. "Look… at…me," he growls.

Darlene stammers. "How are you still alive?"

"I told you already, Sunflower. I'm a new man now. One that can't be killed. The Devil made certain of it the night he saved me. And my new daddy's got plans for me."

"What do you want from me?"

Leroy traces the shape of her lips with his thumb. The tendons in his cheek flex, stiffening what little of his jaw remains. "I want us to be a family again. Start over. Do things right this time. I'll continue to clothe you, shelter you, pay your bills—you won't have to bartend no more. We can be a proper couple, one all the townsfolk will admire."

Darlene starts to cry. "You're sick, Leroy."

"No, Darlene. I am *restored. "* he hisses. "There was a sickness in my heart, I know. But look at me now. Look at *us*." Leroy cups her cheek. "You are my destiny, and I'm yours. You know that, don't you? This is our second chance."

"Stop it, Leroy!"

"LEROY'S DEAD! I'M HATCHET NOW!" Leroy bellows, "All I wanted was for you to love me, Darlene. It was supposed to be you and me, against the world, in our little farmhouse with a couple of kids."

Darlene shudders with fear. "I'm sorry I couldn't save him," she says.

"Don't…" Leroy's anger suddenly melts from his face, replaced by a look of confusion. He loosens his grip on her wrists.

"I tried to save him," she whispers. "I wanted *so* bad to save him."

"Liar…"

"I'm not lyin', Leroy."

Leroy balls his shaking hand into a fist and strikes Darlene so hard across the face, she's certain he shattered her jaw. "You let them take him!" he shouts. "You let them rip him from your body!"

"After you beat me half to death!" Darlene spits blood at Leroy's face. His eyes flash with hellfire, and the next thing Darlene feels is her skull being slammed down onto the floor. Leroy grabs the dull paring knife she had dropped and presses it hard into her forehead, then drags it slow and deep down across her right eye and cheek, all the way to her chin. Darlene screams at the painful loss of vision in her eye.

"There," Leroy says. "Now you look just as pretty as me." He smiles to show off his scars. "You're mine again, Sunflower. Only mine. Till death do us part."

Suddenly, a flash of gray and a rabid hiss throws Leroy off kilter, causing him to fall backward off Darlene and make him wail in pain.

Levi!

Darlene gets up and sees Leroy trying to wrestle Levi's rodent body off his face, but it's no use. Levi's claws are dug in deep. The opossum bites down on Leroy's nose with his sharp little teeth and thrashes back and forth until he rips the scarred cartilage clean off. All that remains is an empty cavity in the middle of Leroy's face.

Seeing his nose in Levi's mouth does something to Leroy, twists his face into something even more monstrous than it was before. He grabs the opossum by the scruff of its neck and hurls it against the wall.

"No!" Hysterical now, Darlene stumbles over to her boy and holds him in her arms. His fur is covered in blood and liquor, and his chest heaves with the weight of a boulder.

Levi lifts his snout. He looks at Darlene with swollen eyes and blinks once. A tremor courses through his body, and Darlene's own flesh responds in kind.

"Not you, too," she whispers, doing her best to fix his little cowboy hat. She wants to put a smile on her face, because she wants to tell Levi everything will be okay, but Levi's smarter than that—always has been.

So, instead, Darlene just lets herself cry.

But when she sees that Leroy is distracted by the hole in his face, trying desperately to reattach the amputated cartilage by pressing it hard enough against the nasal bone, she sees her one chance to escape. With Levi cradled in her arms, she gets to her feet and sprints toward the back hallway.

Leroy sees her make a run for it. He can't, won't let her get away now. He drops his severed nose and stumbles as fast as he can after her.

"All you ever do is leave me!"

A LICK AND A PROMISE

DARLENE REACHES THE bathroom right as the ceiling behind her collapses into a flaming heap of debris. She knows this won't stop Leroy, but it might slow him down just enough.

She carries Levi into the bathroom and locks the door behind them. The smell of death is unbearable. She tries not to look at Ezra's mutilated corpse as she sets Levi in the sink and pushes the dresser in front of the bathroom door as a barricade.

Moments later, the door splinters apart behind her.

Thwack! goes the hatchet.

"I won't let you go again!" Leroy shouts from the other side of the door.

Thwack!

"I'd rather you die than let that happen!"

Thwack!

Leroy grabs the splintered wood and rips it out of the door. He peeks through the small hole left behind like a disfigured Jack Nicholson.

Leroy was a piece of shit. Irredeemable. But Darlene loved him, once. So, as a small mercy, she'd make this quick, even if he didn't deserve it.

The thing about Leroy was that he was a reactive type of man. Darlene knew that; knew Leroy would follow her to the very end. She wanted him to think she would try to run away one last time by escaping through the bathroom window.

But that was never the plan…

…At least not the entirety.

See, when you live with an abusive piece of shit, you learn to be ever vigilant, always on guard, and hyper-observant of your surroundings. And growing up in the Texas Hill Country, Darlene learned that sometimes to catch a predator, your best bet is to set a trap.

She only caught a glimpse of Ezra's dead body the first time she entered this bathroom, back when she was attempting to escape with Orville, but a glimpse was enough. She saw in that moment that the killer had not taken Ezra's pistol. It was still holstered at the old cowboy's hip. If she could get to it before Leroy knew any better, then lure him in after her by pretending to be trapped, she'd have her shot. Literally.

Darlene looks into Leroy's eyes peering through the hole in the door one last time and sighs. Empty. Without soul. The man she once knew was nowhere to be found.

"Sorry, sugar," she says cocking the trigger. "It's not me. It's you." And before Leroy can react, she presses the barrel of Ezra's pistol against one of those ice-blue eyeballs and pulls the trigger. Blood and brain matter splatter the wall behind him, and his body drops from Darlene's sight.

LIFELINE

DARLENE SITS ON the side of the road with Levi asleep in her lap, sipping from a bottle of the finest Kentucky bourbon on The Teegarden's menu. Someone must have tried to swipe it during all the chaos but dropped it in the fields during their escape.

"Worst shift of my life," Darlene says to Levi, stroking the wiry fur on his back. "But I think it's finally over."

Levi opens his eyes and mewls at her.

"I know, I know. I just wanted a moment of peace before we called for help. Lucky for us…"

Darlene reaches down into her jeans pocket and tugs at Brandy's oversized iPhone until it breaks free from the tight denim. She'd taken the phone from Brandy's corpse after escaping through the bathroom window with Levi.

She holds the cell phone to the sky. The case is hot-pink and bedazzled with rhinestones, a design style Darlene has grown to hate, but it also has excellent reception. Three bars of service pop up.

As her fingers pad the buttons for 9-1-1, another plan occurs to her. One that makes her smirk. "Fuck it, why not?" She searches through Brandy's contacts until she finds the name she's looking for: Alma Barrera.

It's three o'clock in the morning, but Alma picks up on the first ring.

Darlene puts her on speaker.

"Brandy?" Alma's voice is garbled, prone to dropping in and out, but the signal remains strong enough to convey the young woman's panic. Three service bars drop down to two. "It's the middle of the night. Is everything okay?"

"No," Darlene says coolly. "I can't say that it is."

The phone goes silent for a moment.

"Who is this?" Alma finally asks.

"Darlene Boone. The bartender."

"Darlene? What's going on? Where's Brandy?"

Only one service bar now.

"We can talk about that another time," says Darlene. "Look, it's been a hell of a night, and right now, I need a favor."

"I—I don't understand…"

"I don't need you to understand. I just need you hang up this phone and call the police—if you'd be so kind. Hell, call the national guard, if you're able. I've got quite the mess to clean up out here at The Teegarden, and I can use all the help I can get."

"You're not making any sense," Alma says as she shuffles to get dressed and grab her keys. "Don't move. I'm heading over there right now."

"Oh, don't you worry." Darlene takes another swig from the bourbon "I'm not going anywhere. I'm staying right here."

TONIGHT'S SETLIST !!!

Son of a Witch
—Justin Johnson

Beer Never Broke My Heart
—Luke Combs

Dios Bendijo Tejas
—Kieth Nieto, Sunny Sauceda, Rico Gonzalez

Stay a Little Longer
—Brothers Osborne

Dumb Blonde
—Dolly Parton

Whiskey River
—Willie Nelson

Too Hard to Say I'm Sorry
—Charley Pride

Psycho   —Jack Kittel

Something to Talk About
—Bonnie Raitt

Neon Moon
—Brooks & Dunn

A Bar Song (Tipsy)
—Shaboozey

When It Rains
—Eli Young Band

The Devil Went Down
to Georgia
—The Charlie Daniels Band

It Wasn't God Who Made
Honky Tonk Angels   —Kitty Wells

Heartless   —Camille Parker

Don't Come Home A-Drinkin'
(With Lovin' On Your Mind)
—Loretta Lynn

Stay in Your Lane —Bronson Diamond,
Greta Stanley

Pass Me By (If You're Only
Passing Through) —Johnny Rodriguez

Texas Hold 'Em
—Beyoncé

THE TEEGARDEN SALOON
KIMBLE COUNTY, TEXAS

my personal playlist:

I know it won't work -Gracie Abrams

Mean Streak - Next of Kin

Blame Brett - The Beaches

Here You Come Again -Dolly Parton

Slim Pickins -Sabrina Carpenter

Someone in This Room -Jesse Murph, Bailey Zimmerman

I Hate Texas - Tanner Adell

Cardinal -Kacey Musgraves

God Needs the Devil -Jonah Kagen

Oklahoma Smokeshow -Zach Bryan

I Wound Easy -Dolly Parton

Use Me -Zach Top

80s Mercedes -Maren Morris

Freedom Was a Highway -Jimmie Allen, Brad Paisley

That Ain't No Man That's The Devil -Jessie Murph

Neon Tears -Camille Parker

1973 Slasher Movie - Ivy James

Pretty Girls -Reneé Rapp

Slow Burn -Kacey Musgraves

XOXO
-Darlene

ACKNOWLEDGMENTS

I DIDN'T GROW up in Texas, but I did grow up in a small town in southern New Jersey, off the Delaware River. A place along the Riverline you wouldn't necessarily get off at. A place where, somehow, everyone knew your business while minding their own. New Jersey's got a flavor all of its own, and as we drove down I-35 in the summer of 2020, I wondered how a Jersey girl like me would fare in big ol' Texas.

That's when I saw the neon moon: a cheeky beaver shining proud above the highway at the largest gas station I'd ever seen.

You see, even though I didn't grow up in Texas, it was my home for four years. I'd learned that Texans aren't so different from the fine folks of New Jersey. They're loud. They like good food. They're all about family and protecting their own. And while I lived there, I made friends with some pretty swell people, whom I affectionately call The Texas Horror Crew. They taught me that Texans aren't a monolith. You can enjoy your cowboy boots and fight for civil liberties. And what I had come to know is the beauty of Central Texas, the magic of San Antonio, and the inescapable wonder and mystery that is the Texas Hill Country, a place that makes you feel both free and very small.

The number of people I'd like to thank for supporting the creation and publication of this book is innumerable, so I will try to keep this short. But first, I'd like to thank my editor and publisher, Rob Carroll. I'm so grateful you saw the story for what it could be and became my battle buddy in gore. It still means a great deal to me that my first pro-publication short story was through *Dark Matter Magazine,* and the publication of *Neon Moon* feels like one of those full-circle kind of moments. Thank you for believing in my writing and daring me to be fearless with my work. I am a better writer and storyteller because of you!

To Katerina Belikova, дякую for designing the cover art for *Neon Moon.* Thank you for bringing The Teegarden Saloon to life and creating the creepiest cowgirl to grace this cover!

To the Texas Horror Crew: You know who you are, and I'm ever thankful for your friendship, even if I now live 1,600 miles away from you.

To The Last Call Crew, thank you for celebrating and promoting *Neon Moon* before and after its release. There's no one else I'd rather survive a honky tonk slasher with than you!

To Ravven White, Wendy Dalrymple, Shannon Stephan, Damien Casey, and Emily Ruth Verona, who beta-read parts of this book in its earliest stages and didn't shriek after reading the first drafts.

To Ashley Calvin, who saw this book through with me back when *Neon Moon* was just a concept under a different name. Thank you for workshopping southern colloquialisms, musical playlists, and social media aesthetics to get the vibes just right. Your Tennessee charm really came through.

To Kayleigh Creates for illustrating the most adorable and badass rendition of Levi, I hope everyone supports your artwork and creative endeavors in the horror community.

To Erin Al-Mehairi, Melissa Nowark, Julia Lewis, Amanda Doscher, Tori A., Amber M., Tessa Marlatt, Laura P., Stephanie M., and Emmy C. for your continued support in my writing endeavors.

And to you, dear reader, for taking the time to read this book! Whatever you read, wherever you go, I hope you always know the freedom of an open road.

—Grace R. Reynolds

ABOUT THE AUTHOR

 **GRACE R. REYNOLDS** is an American speculative fiction writer. She was raised in New Jersey and graduated from Rutgers University. Having lived in seven states, she currently calls Maryland "home," where she writes dark fiction and poetry. In addition to her short fiction, she is the author of *Lady of the House* and two other collections of poetry. These include *The Lies We Weave*, which was nominated for the SFPA Elgin Awards, and *Midnight Blue*. To learn more visit gravereynolds.com.

www.ingramcontent.com/pod-product-compliance
Lightning Source LLC
Chambersburg PA
CBHW021324060726
47591CB00006B/1856